Shadows At Misty Cove

To uncover the truth, she'll have to trust the man who buried it.

Trevor Jensen

Dedication

In the fog of the past, it can be hard to see the way forward.

This is for those who hold onto the belief that truth, like love, is a light that will eventually, and always, break through.

Introduction

Some towns forget. Misty Cove remembers.

It remembers in the mournful cry of the gulls that circle the black, jagged cliffs. It remembers in the way the fog rolls in off the Atlantic, a cold, grey shroud that swallows the shore and muffles the world in a damp, conspiratorial silence. It remembers in the foundations of the salt-bleached houses, in the brittle whispers of its oldest residents, and in the deep, dark water of the cove itself.

Secrets here don't die. They seep into the soil and mingle with the brine. They become ghosts that haunt the docks at midnight and stories that are never told but are understood by all.

Ten years ago, the town made a silent pact. It took its most terrible secret—the one about the girl with the wild laugh who walked into the mist and never came back—and it buried it deep. They covered it with years of routine, with averted gazes and unspoken agreements, hoping the relentless tide would eventually wash the memory away for good.

But the tide always turns. And it always brings back what was lost.

Now, a car is heading down the single coastal highway back into town, carrying a woman with the past in her eyes and the truth on her lips. She is coming home to unravel the one story that was never finished.

And Misty Cove is waiting. It remembers her, too. And it remembers the cost of breaking a promise made in the shadows.

Contents

Chapter 1: Homecoming in the Fog

The fog rolled into Misty Cove exactly as Julia remembered, not with the gentle romance of a movie but with the cold, damp grip of a shroud. It crept over the harbor, swallowing the masts of fishing boats and muffling the lonely cry of the gulls. It clung to the eaves of the salt-bleached buildings on Main Street and slicked the asphalt of the single road leading into a town that was better at keeping secrets than it was at keeping people.

Julia Hart gripped the steering wheel of her sensible sedan, her knuckles white. Ten years. It had been ten years since she had fled this place, trading the scent of brine and decay for the electric hum of the city. She had built a career on digging up other people's secrets, writing stories that were sharp, clean, and blessedly impersonal. But the secret she left behind had festered. It had a name: Sarah Jenkins. And it was the one story she had never been able to write.

Now, she was back. Not as the scared, guilt-ridden girl who ran, but as a reporter with a national byline and a reputation for breaking impenetrable cases. This time, she wouldn't leave until she had the truth.

She parked in front of the Tidewater Market, the bell above the door issuing a tinny, accusing jingle. Inside, the air was thick with the smell of sawdust and dried herbs. Mrs. Gable, a woman whose face seemed permanently puckered from a diet of lemons and gossip, looked up from behind the counter. Her eyes, small and dark like currants, widened for a fraction of a second before a familiar curtain of coastal indifference dropped.

"Julia," she said. The name was a flat statement of fact, devoid of warmth. "Heard you were coming back."

"News travels fast," Julia replied, her voice brighter than she felt. She grabbed a basket, the worn wicker scraping against her practical trench coat.

"Always does, in a town this small." Mrs. Gable began polishing an already gleaming countertop with a gray rag. "Some things are better left buried, you know."

The warning was as subtle as a swinging anchor. Julia forced a smile, grabbing a bottle of water and a protein bar.

She didn't need a welcome party, but the immediate chill confirmed her suspicions. The town hadn't forgotten. It had just perfected its silence.

Her next stop was a small cottage set back from the road, almost consumed by a riot of overgrown roses and ivy. A thin curl of smoke rose from the stone chimney. This was the one place in Misty Cove that had never felt like a trap.

Grace Lockwood opened the door before Julia had even knocked. She was a tiny woman, her silver hair pulled into a messy bun that defied gravity, her face a roadmap of fine lines etched by laughter and wisdom. She was the town's retired librarian, and in Julia's youth, her home had been a sanctuary of books and quiet understanding.

"I felt a disturbance in the fog," Grace said, her eyes twinkling as she pulled Julia into a fierce hug that smelled of old paper and chamomile tea. "Knew it had to be you."

Inside, the cottage was a cozy chaos of stacked books, half-finished cups of tea, and curiosities collected over a lifetime. Grace bustled to the kitchen. "The town's already buzzing. You've stirred the silt at the bottom of the pond, my dear."

"That was the plan," Julia said, sinking into a worn armchair. The exhaustion of the drive was finally setting in, a leaden weight in her bones.

Grace returned with two steaming mugs. "They'll fight you. This town protects its own, even the guilty. Especially the guilty." She settled opposite Julia, her gaze sharp. "They think if they don't speak of the darkness, it can't touch them."

"It already did," Julia said quietly. "It touched Sarah."

"And you," Grace added softly. "And Alec Mason."

The name landed in the space between them, heavy and unwelcome. Julia's jaw tightened. "I'm not here for him."

"Are you sure?" Grace asked, her voice gentle. "Sometimes the story you think you're chasing isn't the one you need to find."

Before Julia left, Grace pressed a small, smooth stone into her hand. "For courage," she whispered, her fingers closing over Julia's. Her expression turned serious. "The tide is turning, my dear. But be careful what it washes ashore. This town is full of people who would rather let a body sink than admit it was ever here at all."

Julia drove toward the marina, telling herself it was the most logical place to get her bearings. A lie. She was looking for him. She had to see what a decade of shared guilt had done to him. The marina was his territory now. He had given up his detective's badge not long after the case went cold, trading the sterile halls of the police station for the raw, physical labor of mending boats and nets. An act of penance, she had always thought.

The fog was thicker here, the air heavy with the groan of wooden docks and the slap of water against hulls. And then she saw him. Alec Mason.

He was standing at the end of a long pier, his back to her. Even from a distance, he was unmistakable. Taller than she remembered, broader through the shoulders. His dark hair was tousled by the damp wind. He was staring out at the grey, churning water, a man locked in a silent, unending battle. In his hands, he held a piece of driftwood and a small knife. Even from a distance, Julia could see the slow, methodical movement of his hands as he carved, shaving slivers of pale wood that were instantly snatched away by the wind. It was a habit he'd had even back then—a way of whittling his anxiety into something smooth, something manageable. Seeing it now felt like a punch to the gut. Some things hadn't changed at all.

For a moment, Julia's hand hovered over the door handle. A storm of unresolved emotions churned inside her: anger, regret, and a deep, aching phantom of the affection they had once shared. He had been the lead detective on Sarah's case. He had been her anchor in the initial storm of grief. And then, he had been the one to tell her it was over. Case closed. No leads. No hope. He had failed Sarah. He had failed her.

He turned his head slightly, as if he could feel her watching him. Julia's breath caught. She ducked her head and quickly put the car in reverse, tires crunching on the gravel as she pulled away before he could see her. One ghost at a time, she told herself. First, Sarah. Alec would have to wait.

Her feet, acting on a memory older than reason, carried her to the town memorial. It was a small, neglected plot of land overlooking the sea, centered on a granite slab engraved with the names of those lost to the cove's treacherous waters. At the bottom, a smaller, newer plaque had been added ten years ago.

Sarah Jenkins. Forever in our hearts.

Julia traced the cold, carved letters with her fingertips. The memory ambushed her, not as a vague fog of sadness, but as a series of sharp, sensory jolts. The sound of Sarah's laugh, a wild, breathless cackle that always made Julia feel brave. The salty-sweet smell of the taffy they'd shared on the boardwalk just hours before she disappeared, the sticky paper warm from the sun. The feel of Sarah's friendship bracelet—woven threads of blue and silver—brushing against Julia's wrist as she'd leaned in to whisper a secret about a boy she liked.

"He looks at you, you know," Sarah had said, her voice giddy. *"Like you're the only person on the whole beach."*

Guilt, cold and acidic, coiled in her stomach. Sarah had been focused on Julia's potential happiness in the moments before her own was extinguished forever. That was the memory that truly haunted her. Her last words to Sarah had been a flippant, "See you tomorrow." The promise had hung in the air for ten years, broken and rotting. She pulled her battered leather notebook from her bag, the pages filled with notes, timelines, and theories. This was more than a story now. It was a debt.

As she turned to leave, a piece of paper tucked under her car's windshield wiper caught her eye. It wasn't a parking ticket. It was a folded note, the paper already growing soft in the damp air. Her hands trembled slightly as she opened it.

The message was typed in a plain, stark font.

Some secrets are anchors. They don't just hold you in place. They pull you down. Go home.

A cold dread washed over her, colder than the sea spray on her face. It was a direct threat. The town wasn't just silent. It was hostile. Someone was watching her. Someone knew why she was here. For the first time that day, a sliver of fear pierced her determination. She crumpled the note in her fist and got back in the car, her heart hammering against her ribs.

She drove the short distance to her childhood home, a two-story clapboard house her mother still kept, preserved in a state of hopeful waiting. The air inside was stale with memories. She dropped her keys on the hall table, the clatter echoing in the stillness. All she wanted was a hot shower and a moment to quiet the noise in her head.

But as she reached for the front door to lock it, she saw it.

Impaled on the dark wood by a single, rusty nail was a small, silver heart. It was tarnished with age, a delicate chain trailing from its clasp. Julia's blood ran cold. She would have known it anywhere. She had given it to Sarah for her sixteenth birthday.

It was Sarah's locket. And it was nailed to her door like a death warrant.

Chapter 2: Unfinished Conversations

The world narrowed to the locket in her hand. It was cold, unnervingly so, as if it had absorbed the chill of the grave Sarah was never granted. Julia's fingers tightened around the tarnished silver heart, the sharp edge of the nail's entry point digging into her palm. For a moment, she was paralyzed by a tidal wave of ice-cold fear. This wasn't a random warning. This was intimate. It was a violation meant to unearth the one thing she had tried to bury for a decade: her own terror.

Then, a different kind of heat flooded her veins. Anger. White-hot and clarifying. Fear was what they wanted. It was the weapon this town had used to silence itself for ten years. She would not let it work on her.

With a wrenching motion, she tore the locket from the door. A long splinter of dark, painted wood came with it. She slammed the heavy door shut, the sound booming through the quiet house, and threw the deadbolt. The click echoed like a gunshot.

"Julia? What on earth was that?"

Her mother's voice drifted from the kitchen, thin and frayed with anxiety. Julia slipped the locket and its cruel nail into the deep pocket of her trench coat, the weight a grim reminder against her hip. She took a deep breath, schooling her features into a mask of calm she was far from feeling.

She found her mother, Eleanor Hart, standing by the sink, her hands twisting a dish towel. Eleanor was a woman who seemed to have shrunk since Julia last saw her, her shoulders permanently stooped as if bracing against a blow that had landed long ago and never stopped echoing.

"Just the wind, Mom," Julia lied.

Eleanor's eyes, the same sharp blue as Julia's but clouded with a perpetual worry, scanned her daughter's face. "The wind doesn't throw deadbolts. What's happened?" Her gaze flicked to the front door, then back to Julia. "This is a mistake. Coming back here."

"I had to," Julia said, her voice tight. She walked past her mother to the coffeemaker, the motions of making a pot familiar and grounding. "The story was never finished."

"It's not a story!" Eleanor's voice cracked, the carefully constructed dam of her composure breaking. "It's our life. It's Sarah, a girl who is gone. It's this town, which almost broke in two. What do you think you're going to find that a dozen police officers, that Alec Mason, couldn't?"

Julia flinched at his name but didn't turn from the counter. "Maybe something they weren't looking for. Maybe a truth people wanted to stay hidden."

"Or maybe you'll just tear open wounds that have barely scarred over," Eleanor shot back, her voice trembling. "For what? A byline? To prove something to people who don't matter?" She stepped closer, her tone dropping to a desperate whisper. "Your father... his heart gave out a year after you left. The stress of it all, the not knowing, seeing you so broken... I can't go through that again, Julia. I can't lose you, too."

The words were a direct hit, aimed with the precision only a mother could manage. Guilt, sharp and suffocating, rose in Julia's throat. "This isn't about a byline, and it's not fair to bring Dad into this."

"Isn't it?" Eleanor's face was pale. "This town took Sarah. It took your father. It took my daughter and sent a stranger back in her place. Don't let it take what's left."

The air crackled with a decade of things unsaid. Julia wanted to scream that she hadn't been a stranger, she'd been a drowning girl. She wanted to say that staying would have been its own kind of death. Instead, she just shook her head, the coffee pot now gurgling between them.

"I'm not the same girl who left, Mom. I know how to handle myself. And I'm not leaving until I know what happened to my friend." Her voice was quiet but laced with steel. It was a declaration of war, and from the defeated look on her mother's face, she knew she had won the battle, even if it felt like losing.

Leaving her mother in a tense, wounded silence, Julia retreated upstairs to the one place that was unequivocally hers: her childhood bedroom. It was a time capsule. Faded band posters were still taped to the walls, a stack of noir paperbacks teetered on her nightstand, and a fine layer of dust coated everything. The air was still and close, thick with the ghosts of teenage dreams and anxieties. This was where she and Sarah had spent countless hours, whispering secrets, planning their futures, and believing they were invincible.

She sank onto the edge of the bed, the mattress groaning in protest. She needed a new lead, something untouched by ten years of official neglect. Something only she might recognize. Her eyes scanned the room and landed on a heavy wooden chest at the foot of her bed. Her "archives."

She lifted the lid. The scent of old paper and cedar wafted out. Inside were stacks of yearbooks, concert ticket stubs, and her own journals. She pulled out the one from that final year, its leather cover worn smooth. Her handwriting was a frantic, loopy scrawl back then. She flipped through the pages, a chronicle of teenage angst and high school drama, until she reached the week of the Founder's Day bonfire.

Most entries were what she expected: complaints about classes, excitement for the weekend. But then she found it. An entry from three days before Sarah disappeared.

October 28. Fought with S again. She's been so weird lately. Jumpy. Said she had to do something she didn't want to do. Something about making things right. When I asked what, she just said, 'The tide comes for everyone, Jules. You either learn to swim, or you build a better boat.' Sounded like something her dad would say. She wouldn't tell me more. She looked scared.

Julia stared at the page. She remembered the fight, but she had dismissed it as typical teenage melodrama. Reading it now, the words felt sinister. *Making things right.* What had Sarah done that needed correcting? And the phrase... *The tide comes for everyone.* It was an old fisherman's saying, one she'd heard a hundred times in Misty Cove. But coming from Sarah, who hated the town's folksy fatalism, it was jarring.

It was a thread. Thin, frayed, but it was a start.

A loud, cheerful shout from downstairs broke her concentration. "Special delivery for the world-famous investigative journalist!"

A smile touched Julia's lips for the first time that day. Finn.

She met him on the landing. Her cousin was a whirlwind of energy, all lanky limbs and a grin that seemed too big for his face. He was carrying a crate filled with tech gear.

"Figured you'd need a proper war room," Finn said, nudging her aside to carry the crate into her bedroom. "Got your laptop, a secure router so the local yokels can't spy on your Wi-Fi, a police scanner app for my phone, and... ta-da!" He produced a bag of her favorite salt and vinegar chips. "Brain food."

"You're a lifesaver, Finn," she said, the tension in her shoulders easing a fraction. Finn was family, but he was also her staunchest ally, the only person who had never questioned her obsession with the case.

He began hooking up cables, his easy chatter filling the dusty silence. "So, Mom told me Aunt Eleanor is already in Defcon 1. Said you're 'kicking the hornet's nest'."

"She's not wrong," Julia admitted, leaning against the doorframe.

"Good." Finn's expression turned serious for a moment. "It's about time someone did. This place has felt haunted for too long." He looked around the room, at the ghosts on the walls. "You okay being back in here?"

"It's where the work needs to happen," she said, evading the real question.

Suddenly, a shadow fell across the doorway. Both of them looked up. Alec Mason was standing there. The air in the room instantly became thin.

Finn, sensing the sudden deep freeze, cleared his throat. "Well, look at that, I think I, uh, left the... thing... in the car. Be right back." He practically dove out of the room, leaving them alone in a silence that was suddenly suffocating.

Alec's eyes flicked from the nail hole in the front door, visible from the landing, back to her. "I saw your car," he said, his voice a low rumble that vibrated through the floorboards and straight up Julia's spine. "I had to see if you were..." He trailed off, his jaw working as if the words themselves were a struggle.

"I'm fine," she said, her voice clipped. It was a pathetic lie, and they both knew it. She hated how he could still make her feel so transparent. "What do you want, Alec?"

Instead of answering, he moved. He didn't just step into the room; he seemed to consume the space, closing the distance until he stood directly in front of her. The air grew thick, charged with the scent of him—motor oil, salt, and the clean, woodsy smell of the flannel shirt he wore. It was the same scent that had once clung to her own clothes, a scent she had associated with safety and a desperate, thrilling first love. Her body remembered it before her mind could protest.

Her breath hitched. She had to tilt her head back slightly to meet his gaze, and she hated the flicker of vulnerability it exposed. His eyes, those haunted hazel eyes, weren't just angry or worried. They were searching hers, filled with a decade of questions he'd never asked.

"I want you to be careful," he said, his voice now a low, intense murmur that was for her alone. He was so close she could feel the warmth radiating from his body. Every nerve ending she possessed was screamingly aware of him.

"I know how to be careful," she retorted, but her voice lacked its usual bite.

"No, you don't," he countered, a muscle feathering in his cheek. "Not here. You come back like a storm, thinking you can just tear the truth out of the ground. But you're not just prying at the town's secrets, Julia. You're prying at mine." His gaze dropped to her mouth for a fraction of a second, and the air crackled. "And yours."

He lifted a hand, his calloused fingers hesitating in the space between them. For a dizzying moment, she thought he was going to touch her—tuck a stray strand of hair behind her ear, trace the line of her jaw—the way he used to. Her pulse hammered in her throat, a frantic, traitorous beat. Part of her leaned into the imagined touch, craving it like a drug. The other part of her screamed to shove him away.

But he let his hand drop, balling it into a fist at his side. The moment shattered.

"You closed the case," she whispered, the accusation a shield against the dizzying pull of his presence.

The warmth in his eyes vanished, replaced by a familiar, shuttered pain. "There were no more leads."

"Or you stopped looking."

"That's not fair," he said, his voice raw. "You have no idea what I did. What I lost." He finally took a step back, and Julia could breathe again, though the air felt cold and empty where he had been standing. "Just... don't trust anyone. Not the cops. Not Crane. No one."

He gave a final, tormented look, turned, and was gone. Julia stood frozen, her hand pressed to her chest as if to calm her racing heart. She was furious with him for his warnings, for his hypocrisy, for his secrets. But she was even more furious with herself for the simple, undeniable truth: a single look from Alec Mason could still unravel her completely.

Shaking her head, she turned back to her work. She had to focus. She began unpacking the box of files she'd brought from the city—a decade's worth of obsessive research. Old newspaper clippings, copies of redacted police reports she'd acquired through official channels, maps of the area.

She laid them out on her old desk, creating a mosaic of tragedy. As she lifted a stack of articles, a single sheet of paper that wasn't hers slipped out and drifted to the floor. It was a photocopy, the ink slightly faded.

Her blood turned to ice. It was a witness statement from the original investigation. A statement from Ruby Santiago, the town gossip, claiming she'd seen a dark sedan near the bonfire path. Julia knew this statement well; it had been officially discredited and sealed when Ruby changed her story a week later, claiming she'd been mistaken. Julia had only ever read the redacted summary. This was the full, unabridged text.

Someone had access to sealed police files.

Her eyes scanned to the bottom of the page. Below the official signature line, there was a handwritten message in neat, deliberate block letters.

YOU'RE NOT THE ONLY ONE WHO REMEMBERS. SOME OF US NEVER FORGOT.

The threat was no longer on her doorstep. It was here. In her room. Among her most private files. They hadn't just been watching her. They had been waiting for her.

Chapter 3: Ghosts of the Boathouse

Midnight in Misty Cove was a liquid darkness, thick and unnervingly silent. The fog had retreated, leaving behind a sky littered with cold, distant stars and a moon that cast everything in shades of silver and ash. It was the kind of night where ghosts felt not only possible, but probable.

Julia moved through the shadows, her sneakers silent on the damp pine needles lining the path. The crumpled photocopy of Ruby Santiago's statement was a burning coal in her pocket. Ruby had claimed to see a sedan near the path to the old boathouse, a detail that had been conveniently forgotten when the police dismissed her testimony. The boathouse had been a derelict relic even when Julia was a teenager, a place of dares and whispered secrets, its floorboards sticky with spilled beer and salt rot. It was exactly the kind of place Sarah, with her love for the dramatic and the forgotten, might have gone to meet someone.

The structure loomed ahead, a skeletal silhouette against the water. Its roof sagged, and the windows were dark, vacant eyes. The air grew heavy with the smell of decay, of wet, rotting wood and the stagnant, fishy scent of low tide. Every creak of a branch, every slap of water against the pilings below, sent a fresh jolt of adrenaline through her. She wasn't the same girl who had run from this town, she reminded herself, her hand closing around the cold metal of a small, powerful flashlight. She was a reporter chasing a lead.

She reached the weathered door, its blue paint peeling away to reveal grey, splintered wood beneath. It was latched with a heavy, rusted padlock. Amateurs, she thought, pulling a set of lock picks from a slim case in her jacket. A skill she'd picked up for a story on cat burglars and had found surprisingly useful ever since. She inserted the tension wrench, her touch delicate, listening for the faint click of the tumblers.

One pin set. Then another. She was concentrating so fiercely that she didn't hear the footsteps behind her until it was too late.

A hand clamped down on her shoulder. Hard.

A strangled cry escaped her throat. She spun around, dropping the picks and swinging her flashlight like a club. It connected with a solid forearm, and a man grunted in pain. She didn't wait to see his face. She bolted, crashing through the overgrown bushes at the side of the path. Branches clawed at her face and clothes. Her heart hammered against her ribs, a wild drumbeat of pure panic.

He was fast. In three long strides, he caught the back of her jacket, pulling her off balance. She stumbled, falling to one knee as he spun her around and pinned her against the rough wall of the boathouse. A large, calloused hand covered her mouth, stifling her scream.

"Julia, stop! It's me!"

The voice was a harsh, frantic whisper in her ear. Alec. Her struggles ceased, her body going rigid with a different kind of shock. He was breathing heavily, his chest pressed against her back. He smelled of the night and the sea.

Slowly, he removed his hand from her mouth but didn't release her. His other arm was still a steel band around her, holding her pinned. "What the hell are you doing here?" he demanded, his voice a low, angry growl.

"Let go of me!" she hissed, shoving against his immovable frame. She twisted in his grip, finally managing to face him. In the stark moonlight, his face was all sharp angles and furious shadows.

He ignored her struggles, his eyes fixed on the rusted padlock she had been trying to pick. "Ruby Santiago," he said, his voice clipped. "Her statement. That's why you're here, isn't it?"

Julia froze, stunned into silence. How could he know? The question slammed into her with the force of an accusation.

"You're not the only one who can't let this go, Julia," he continued, his gaze finally snapping to hers, burning with an intensity that stole her breath. "And you're not the only one who gets anonymous mail. So, I'll ask you again. What the hell are you doing here, messing with a lead I was already working on?"

The revelation knocked the fight right out of her. He wasn't here for her. Not really. He was here for Sarah. The thought sent a complex, warring mixture of relief and a strange, sharp sting of disappointment through her.

Before she could form a response, a sound cut through the night. The low crunch of tires on the gravel access road.

They both froze, their new, unspoken conflict forgotten. A pair of headlights sliced through the trees, sweeping across the front of the boathouse before cutting out. A car door opened, then closed with a soft, solid thud.

"Get inside," Alec whispered, his voice urgent. He shoved her toward the door, scooping up her lock picks and flashlight.

"The lock..." Julia started.

"There's a bolt on the inside. Go!"

He practically pushed her through the doorway and followed, pulling the heavy door shut behind them. The darkness inside was absolute, a thick, smothering blanket. Alec fumbled for a moment before the rusty scrape of a deadbolt sliding home echoed in the cavernous space. They were plunged into silence, broken only by the sound of their own ragged breathing.

Footsteps sounded on the wooden porch outside. Heavy. Deliberate.

Alec grabbed her arm, pulling her deeper into the boathouse, away from the door. He guided her behind a stack of old, musty lobster traps. They crouched in the narrow space, their bodies pressed together. Julia's back was against the cold, damp wood of the wall, and Alec was a shield of solid warmth in front of her. His hand rested on the wall just beside her head, caging her in. She could feel the steady, powerful beat of his heart, or maybe it was her own. The air was thick with the smell of dust and him.

The footsteps outside stopped. A heavy knock rattled the door. Then another. Julia held her breath, her eyes straining to see in the darkness. A thin sliver of moonlight pierced a grimy window, illuminating the swirling dust motes between them. She could just make out the tense line of Alec's jaw, the grim set of his mouth. He was listening, every muscle in his body coiled and ready.

"We shouldn't have locked it," she whispered, her mouth so close to his ear she could feel the warmth of her own breath bounce back at her. "An unlocked door is just an empty building. A locked one means someone's inside."

"Too late now," he breathed back, his gaze never leaving the door.

The person outside began to move again, the footsteps slow and circling. They passed the grimy window, and for a split second, a hulking shadow blotted out the moonlight. As the shadow moved on, a faint, acrid scent drifted through the cracks in the wall. Stale cigar smoke. It was a smell of stale deals and cheap motels, a scent of decay that had nothing to do with the rotting wood around them. It made the hairs on Julia's arms stand on end.

As they crouched there, trapped in the charged silence, Julia's eyes adjusted further. Her gaze dropped to the floor beside Alec's boot. Something was wedged in a gap between two floorboards. It wasn't a splinter or a random piece of trash. It was rectangular, with a singed, blackened edge.

Carefully, so as not to make a sound, she reached down. Her fingers brushed against his leg, and a jolt, sharp and unwelcome, shot through her. He flinched but didn't move away. Her fingers closed around the object. It was stiff, glossy. A piece of a photograph.

She held it up in the sliver of moonlight. The image was faded and damaged, but the part that remained was horribly clear. It was a picture of four laughing teenagers, illuminated by the flickering orange glow of a bonfire. She recognized herself, younger and impossibly carefree. She recognized Alec, his arm thrown casually around her shoulders. And she recognized a smiling, vibrant Sarah. The fourth person, a boy standing slightly behind Sarah with his hand on her waist, had been mostly burned away. All that remained was a bit of his jacket sleeve and a distinctive silver ring on his finger—a thick band with some kind of crest carved into it.

A jolt went through Julia, entirely separate from the fear of the man outside. The ring. A cold wave of familiarity washed over her. She'd seen that ring before. She knew it. But the memory was a ghost, hovering just at the edge of her mind, refusing to come into focus. Whose was it?

The question was an immediate, maddening itch under her skin.

A gasp escaped her lips, small and sharp. Alec looked down at the photo, his eyes widening.

Outside, the footsteps stopped again, this time directly in front of the door. There was a faint metallic scrape. A key, Julia thought with a fresh wave of panic. But the sound was wrong. It was followed by a grating, squealing noise.

Prying. Someone was trying to pry the door open.

Alec shifted, his body pressing her further into the wall. His hand moved from the wall to her shoulder, a gesture of grim, protective warning. They were trapped. Locked in a decaying tinderbox with the ghosts of the past, while a very real threat was trying to break down the door and join them.

Chapter 4:
Echoes and Alliances

The grating sound of metal on wood was followed by a sharp crack. The door shuddered in its frame. They were out of time.

"The back window," Alec hissed, his voice a blade in the darkness. He was already moving, pulling Julia with him.

They scrambled over a pile of rotting nets and decaying buoys. At the far end of the boathouse, a large window, its glass long gone, offered a view of the black, churning water of the cove. A storm was rolling in, the wind picking up, whipping the surface of the water into a frenzy.

"It's too high," Julia said, her heart leaping into her throat. The drop to the water was at least ten feet.

Another splintering crack came from the front door. It wouldn't hold for much longer.

"It's not a choice," Alec said, already swinging a leg over the sill. He paused, looking back at her. In the sliver of moonlight, his face was a grim mask. "I'll go first. Try to break your fall."

He didn't wait for her agreement. He disappeared over the edge, and she heard the heavy splash a second later. Now it was her turn. She could hear the heavy, frantic breathing of the man outside, fueled by rage and effort. She clambered onto the windowsill, her hands slick with grime. For a terrifying second, she hesitated, staring down at the turbulent water. Then the front door of the boathouse burst open with a final, violent crash.

Julia jumped.

The impact with the water was a brutal, full-body shock. The cold was so intense it felt like fire, stealing the air from her lungs. She went under, disoriented in the blackness, her clothes dragging her down. Strong hands grabbed her, hauling her to the surface. She came up sputtering, gasping for air, Alec holding her steady.

"This way," he ordered, his voice tight from the cold. He was already towing her toward the shore, his powerful strokes cutting through the waves. The water was shallow here, only up to their waists, but the muddy bottom tried to suck the shoes from their feet with every step.

They collapsed onto the rocky beach fifty yards away, hidden by a cluster of jagged rocks. Soaked, shivering, and breathing in ragged gasps, they watched the boathouse. The hulking figure of the man stood in the ruined doorway, a crowbar clutched in his hand. He swept a powerful flashlight beam across the water, the light dancing dangerously close to their position before moving on. He let out a roar of pure frustration that the wind snatched and tore to pieces. After another moment, he turned and stalked back toward his car.

They waited until the red taillights had vanished completely down the access road.

"He knows we were there," Julia said, her teeth chattering. "He knows we saw him."

"Which means nowhere is safe," Alec finished. He looked at her, his face pale, water dripping from his dark hair onto his shoulders. A deep cut was bleeding freely on his forearm where her flashlight had connected with him. "We need to get somewhere warm. Somewhere secure. Grace's."

The walk to Grace's cottage felt like an eternity. The storm broke in earnest, unleashing a torrential, freezing rain. By the time they stumbled onto her porch, they were two half-drowned ghosts, leaving puddles with every step.

Grace opened the door, took one look at their state, and simply said, "In. Now."

She was a whirlwind of calm efficiency, stripping them of their soaked jackets, thrusting thick, dry towels into their hands, and wrapping them in old woolen blankets that smelled of lavender. She sat them in front of the crackling fireplace and returned with two mugs of tea so hot and sweet it burned a trail of life back into Julia's frozen core.

"I'll call Finn," Julia managed, her fingers clumsy on her phone. "He needs to know."

While she relayed a heavily edited version of the night's events to her cousin, telling him to meet them, Grace tended to Alec's arm, cleaning the cut with a steady hand. The quiet intimacy of the act was not lost on Julia. Grace worked, and Alec let her, his usual guard down for just a moment, his face tight with pain.

When Finn arrived ten minutes later, breathless and wide-eyed, the four of them were assembled in Grace's cozy, cluttered living room. The storm raged outside, rattling the windowpanes, a perfect mirror for the tempest in the cottage.

Alec laid the piece of the photograph on the coffee table. It had survived its dunk in the cove, though the edges were now warped.

"Sarah had this?" Grace asked, her voice soft as she peered at the image through her spectacles.

"It was at the boathouse," Julia explained. "Hidden. We think the person who chased us was looking for it."

Finn leaned in close. "Okay, so that's you, Jules. And a surprisingly non-broody Alec. And Sarah. But who's the fourth guy? The one playing grab-ass with Sarah?"

"We don't know," Alec said, his voice gravelly. "His face is gone. All we have is that ring."

Grace squinted at the tiny detail. "A crest... It feels familiar," she said, her gaze distant. She gently pushed the photo away. "But that was a time when people were... very persuasive. After Sarah was gone, it was better for everyone to have a poor memory about certain things. Safer."

The implication sent a chill through Julia that had nothing to do with her damp clothes.

"I'll see what I can find," Finn said, already pulling out his laptop. "Give me a few minutes with the great and powerful Google."

As Finn began typing furiously, Julia's gaze went back to the warped photograph on the table. Before she could reignite her argument with Alec, she found him looking at it too. The anger in his eyes had momentarily softened, replaced by a deep, familiar sadness that mirrored her own.

"She was so happy that night," Julia said, her voice barely a whisper. "Before everything."

"She'd just gotten that scholarship application in," Alec remembered, his voice quiet. "She was convinced she was going to get out."

For a brief, fragile moment, they weren't adversaries. They were just two people staring at a ghost, united by the same gaping hole in their past. The moment was intimate and deeply sad, a reminder of what they had all lost. It was broken when Julia hardened her expression, unwilling to let him see the vulnerability.

"And someone stopped her," she said, her voice now clipped and businesslike. She turned to face him fully. "So, you first. How did you know about Ruby's statement? And what other 'anonymous mail' have you gotten?"

Alec stiffened, pulling the blanket tighter around his shoulders. "I got a package two days ago. No return address. Inside was a copy of the original case file. The whole thing. Including witness statements I was told had been lost."

"The whole file?" Julia's mind reeled. "Why wouldn't you tell me?"

"Tell you what? That someone is playing games with us? That they're trying to turn us against each other by feeding us the same information?" he shot back, his eyes flashing. "I was trying to figure out the angle before I brought you into something even more dangerous."

"I'm already in it!" she said, her voice rising. "That thing with my files, the locket on my door… we are stronger if we work together, Alec! If we actually trust each other."

"Trust?" The word came out as a short, bitter laugh. "You ran, Julia. You packed a bag and you ran away from the wreckage. You left me here to clean it up. Trust doesn't just reappear because you decide to come home ten years later."

The accusation, so raw and specific, struck her speechless. Before she could rally a defense, Finn interrupted, his eyes glued to his screen. "Guys," he said, his tone urgent. "You need to see this."

He pointed to an article on the local news website, posted less than an hour ago. *MAYOR CRANE ISSUES TOWN-WIDE CURFEW CITING PUBLIC SAFETY CONCERNS.*

"Effective immediately," Finn read aloud, "'all residents are to remain indoors from 10 p.m. to 6 a.m. until further notice, due to recent disturbances that threaten the peace of our community.' She's shutting the town down."

"She's boxing us in," Julia breathed. The man at the boathouse, the timing of this announcement... it was all connected. They were being hunted, and now their cage had just gotten smaller.

The tense silence that followed was heavy with unspoken fears. The fire crackled, the storm howled, and the four of them were an island of conspiracy in a town that was actively trying to smother them.

An hour later, the storm had lessened to a steady, miserable drizzle. The tea was gone, and the adrenaline had been replaced by a bone-deep weariness.

"We can't stay here," Alec said, finally rising to his feet. "It puts Grace in danger."

Grace just smiled a little. "This old woman has weathered worse storms than this, son. But you're right. You need to go."

Julia and Alec walked out into the damp, chilled night. The streets were unnervingly empty, a ghost town under the new curfew. As they approached the spot where Julia had left her car, she saw it.

One of her tires was slashed, the rubber sagging sadly to the asphalt. That was bad enough. But it was the word scratched into the driver's side door in deep, vicious gouges that made her blood run cold.

BOATHOUSE.

"He followed us from the cove," she whispered, horrified. "He knows who we are. He knows where I'm staying."

Alec's face was stone. He pulled out his phone, his movements sharp and angry. But before he could dial, Julia's own phone buzzed in her pocket. A blocked number. Her reporter's instincts took over. She answered, putting it on speaker.

At first, there was only static, a harsh, electronic hiss. Then, a voice, distorted and garbled as if filtered through water, broke through the noise.

"...the ring... she never should have taken it..."

The voice dissolved into a burst of static, followed by a soft, chilling sound—the faint, lonely cry of a gull. Then the line went dead.

Julia stared at her phone, her blood like ice in her veins. Beside her, Alec had gone completely still, his face pale. His eyes were narrowed, not in confusion, but with a flicker of disturbed recognition. He knew that sound.

Chapter 5: The Meeting at Sundown

The next day passed in a blur of furious energy and frayed nerves. The vandalized car was a stark, ugly monument to their vulnerability. The garbled phone call echoed in Julia's head, each distorted word a hook she couldn't dislodge. Alec's reaction to the gull's cry was another secret he was keeping, a new brick in the wall between them. He had retreated into a stony, watchful silence, leaving her to pace the confines of her mother's house like a caged animal.

They were being hunted, cornered. The town-wide curfew was a strategic masterstroke, blanketing Misty Cove in a manufactured peace while allowing its shadows to move unchecked. Julia knew she couldn't win this fight by hiding. She had to drag the darkness into the light.

The opportunity came via Finn, who called her late in the afternoon, his voice buzzing with excitement. "They're holding a town meeting. City Hall. Sundown. Mayor Crane wants to 'address the community's concerns' about the curfew."

"It's a trap," Alec said immediately when she told him. He was standing by the window, staring out at the grey, unforgiving sea. "She's going to control the narrative, paint you as the villain, and solidify her grip."

"Then I'll write a new script," Julia retorted, grabbing her jacket. A reckless, desperate plan was forming in her mind. "I'm tired of playing defense. Let's see how they handle a direct attack."

"Julia, don't. This is what they want. A public spectacle they can control."

"They can try." She met his worried, angry gaze in the reflection of the window. "Are you coming, or am I doing this alone?"

He let out a frustrated sigh, the sound of a man caught in a current he couldn't fight. "Like I have a choice."

The Town Hall was a stern, colonial-style building that had always felt more like a courthouse than a community center. As they arrived, the sun was sinking toward the horizon, bathing the town green in a deceptive golden light that did nothing to warm the evening chill. The light turned the windows of the hall into opaque, fiery squares. Alec stopped her before she could reach the door, his hand closing gently on her arm.

"Once you go in there and do this, there's no turning back," he said, his voice low and urgent. "They will come after you with everything they have."

"They already are," she countered, not pulling away from his touch. "The only thing that changes now is I'm fighting back where everyone can see."

"Then be smart in there, Julia. Not just loud."

"Loud is how you get heard, Alec," she replied, her voice softening almost imperceptibly. "You of all people should know how easily quiet gets buried in this town."

She pulled her arm free and pushed through the heavy doors, leaving him to follow in the wake of her determination.

The atmosphere within was thick with a tension that was almost breathable. The room was packed, the heavy wooden pews filled with the familiar faces of Misty Cove. Julia felt their eyes on her as she and Alec walked down the center aisle. There were whispers, a ripple of hostility that followed them like a wake.

Julia watched as Mayor Crane ascended the two steps to the dais, a picture of civic grace. As she settled in her seat, her gaze swept the room and met Chief Ward's. Julia caught it—a flicker of a glance between them, a brief, almost imperceptible nod from Ward to his supposed superior. It wasn't the look of a subordinate acknowledging an order. It was the look of a co-conspirator confirming that the stage was set. A cold knot formed in Julia's stomach.

"Thank you all for coming on such short notice," Crane began, her voice smooth as polished marble. She spoke of unity, of shared values, of the unfortunate necessity of the curfew to ensure the safety of their peaceful home. "We have always been a town that looks after its own. These measures are simply a precaution against outside disturbances that seek to disrupt our harmony."

It was a masterful performance. She was framing Julia as an intruder. Julia's blood boiled. She stood up.

"Mayor Crane," she said, her voice clear and carrying through the suddenly silent hall. "You mention 'disturbances.' Are you referring to the renewed interest in what happened to Sarah Jenkins ten years ago?"

A collective gasp went through the room. Crane's smile tightened. "Ms. Hart. This is a forum for concerned citizens, not a press conference for your... stories."

"I am a concerned citizen," Julia shot back. "My car was vandalized last night. I received a threatening phone call. The locket of a girl who disappeared ten years ago was nailed to my mother's door. Are these the kinds of 'disturbances' your curfew is meant to prevent? Or is it meant to prevent anyone from asking why this case was buried so quickly?"

The whispers erupted into a low roar. Mayor Crane banged her gavel. "That is enough! These are baseless accusations."

Alec rose to his feet, not beside Julia, but a few feet away. He was walking a tightrope, and Julia saw it clearly. He was still angry with her; she could see it in the rigid line of his shoulders. He thought her methods were reckless. But as he spoke, defending her right to ask questions, she also saw a flash of the man he used to be—the fiercely protective detective who believed in justice above all else. There was a grudging admiration in his eyes, and it struck her more deeply than his anger. He was fighting with her, and he was fighting *for* her, all at the same time.

"People are scared, Evelyn," he said, his voice calm and steady. "They see the threats Julia is talking about. They deserve real answers, not platitudes and a lockdown."

Crane's eyes narrowed, her fury now directed at Alec. "Your sentimentality was a liability when you were a detective, Alec, and it's a liability now," she said, her voice dripping with disdain. "Let's be honest. Your family has always had a blind spot where the Harts are concerned. Your judgment is compromised."

The cruelty of the remark, so personal and layered, was stunning. Before Alec could retaliate, a shaky voice rose from the back of the hall.

"She's right! He's right!"

Every head turned. It was Ruby Santiago. Her face was pale, her hands trembling, but her eyes were defiant. "People *are*being threatened!" she cried out. "They're trying to keep us quiet, just like they did back then! I saw something that night, and I was told to forget it, told it was for the best! Told to change my story!"

The admission hung in the air, electric and undeniable. It was the first crack in the dam. The murmuring in the crowd shifted, turning from hostility towards Julia to suspicion towards the dais. Mayor Crane's composure finally fractured, her face a mask of cold rage. She slammed the gavel down again and again. "This meeting is adjourned!"

Chaos erupted as people began talking all at once. As the wave of noise and motion washed over her, Julia felt a firm, warm hand on the small of her back. It was Alec. He had moved to her side in the confusion, his presence a sudden, solid anchor. It wasn't a romantic gesture; it was a protective, instinctual one, a silent message: *I'm here. We're in this together.* The unexpected contact sent a tremor of heat through her, a startling counterpoint to the icy fear gripping the room.

In the crush of bodies moving toward the exits, she felt a different presence beside her. An elderly fisherman she only vaguely recognized pressed a thick, sealed envelope into her hand. As he did, his terrified eyes flicked nervously over his shoulder, directly toward Police Chief Clayton Ward, who was watching the crowd from the dais.

"They're not the only ones who remember," the fisherman rasped, his voice a dry whisper of sea salt and secrets. He was gone before she could even see his face clearly.

Julia looked down at her hand. The envelope was heavy, made of old, creamy stationery. Scrawled across the front in an elegant, spidery script were four words that made her heart stop.

For Your Eyes Only.

Chapter 6: Sheltered by the Storm

The chaos of the town hall spilled out into the rapidly falling dusk. Voices rose and fell in angry, confused eddies as residents argued on the steps. Mayor Crane was already gone, spirited away in a town car, but Julia could feel the lingering weight of her fury, a palpable threat in the air.

"We have to go. Now," Alec said, his hand still a firm, grounding pressure on her back. He guided her through the throng, his broad shoulders clearing a path. He didn't lead her to her vandalized car, but instead cut across the green toward the marina.

"Where are we going?" she asked, her mind still reeling from the fisherman's cryptic message and the heavy weight of the envelope in her hand.

"Your mother's house is the first place they'll watch," he said, his voice grim. "Grace's is compromised. My office is the only place left."

As if on cue, the wind howled, and the drizzle that had plagued the evening intensified into a driving, torrential rain. The sky, which had been a bruised purple, turned a deep, starless black. The storm they had been promised was here, breaking over Misty Cove with a furious, cleansing violence. They ran the last hundred yards, the rain plastering their clothes to their skin, the wind trying to steal the air from their lungs.

Alec's office was a small, self-contained building at the end of the main pier, overlooking the churning harbor. It was his fortress. He fumbled with the key, shoved the door open, and pulled her inside, slamming it shut against the storm's assault.

The sound of the tempest was immediately muffled, reduced to a wild drumming on the roof and a mournful whistle at the window frames. The space was one large room, smelling of sawdust, varnish, and the faint, clean scent of cedar. A workbench littered with tools and half-finished driftwood sculptures took up one wall. A map of the cove's treacherous currents was pinned to another. In the corner, a pot-bellied stove stood cold, and a couple of worn armchairs were angled toward it. It was a space of quiet, masculine solitude.

"Let's see it," Alec said, shrugging out of his wet jacket. He moved to the stove, his motions economical and sure, and began building a fire.

Julia's hands trembled slightly as she broke the seal on the envelope. The paper was thick, expensive. Inside was a single, folded sheet. The same elegant, spidery handwriting covered the page.

I was mending my nets on my boat that night, the letter began, with no preamble. *Everyone was at the bonfire. I saw a car come down the old access road. Not the junker Ruby Santiago drove. This was a new car, a dark green luxury sedan. The kind of car you don't see in Misty Cove, except maybe on a summer tourist. It didn't have its headlights on. It parked near the path to the boathouse for maybe twenty minutes. When it left, it drove fast. I saw part of the license plate under the security light at the marina entrance. It started with LWC. I told an officer what I saw the next day. He told me I must have been mistaken, that it wasn't important. He said it was better not to make waves. I have been silent for ten years. I see you, and I am ashamed.*

"LWC," Julia breathed, staring at the letters.

"A ten-year-old lead about a car no one here could afford," Alec countered, though his eyes were sharp with interest as he read the letter over her shoulder. The fire caught, spitting and crackling to life, casting flickering shadows across his face.

Julia's mind flashed to the other piece of evidence tucked away in her wallet: the fragment of the photograph. "A luxury sedan," she said, thinking out loud. "An expensive-looking ring with a family crest... We're not looking for a fisherman, Alec. We're looking for someone from one of the founding families. Someone with money and power."

He straightened up and walked over to a small cabinet, retrieving a bottle of amber liquid and two glasses. "Whiskey," he said. "We've earned it."

He poured two generous measures, the silence stretching between them, filled only by the fire and the storm. He handed her a glass, their fingers brushing. The brief contact was electric, a jolt of warmth that had nothing to do with the whiskey or the fire.

She took a sip, the fiery liquid chasing the last of the chill from her bones. The events of the last few days, of the last few hours, began to settle. They were trapped here, in this small room, an island in the storm, with the ghosts of the past and the threats of the present swirling outside.

"Your family has always had a blind spot where the Harts are concerned," Julia said quietly, echoing Crane's venomous words. "What did she mean by that?"

Alec swirled the whiskey in his glass. "My grandfather and yours started a fishing business together. It fell apart. Badly. Our families haven't been close since, but there's history. Crane knows that. She knows how to twist any connection into a weapon."

The confession was small, but it was something. A piece of himself he hadn't walled off.

"I remember another storm like this," she said, her voice soft. "The summer before senior year. We all got caught out on the beach. You built a bonfire out of driftwood that smoked more than it burned."

A rare, small smile touched his lips. "And you and Sarah tried to teach me how to dance to some terrible song on the radio, until we were all soaked and laughing too hard to stand." He looked at her, his eyes dark with memory. "Better days."

"Yes," she whispered. "Better days."

The intimacy of the memory hung in the air, fragile and sweet. Before it could dissolve, his pocket buzzed. He pulled out his phone, his expression hardening. "It's Finn. Put you on speaker."

"Okay, you are not going to believe this," Finn's voice came through. "The phone call you got? I isolated the background noise. That gull cry… it's not a gull."

"What is it?" Julia asked, leaning closer.

"It's a recording. Specifically, it's the automated foghorn from the old Point Reyes lighthouse, twenty miles up the coast. The one that was decommissioned fifteen years ago. It had a really unique, two-tone signal. Unmistakable, if you know what you're listening for."

Julia looked at Alec. His face was pale. He knew. Of course he knew. "Why would someone play that?" she asked.

"I don't know," Finn said. "But it's a message. A specific one. I'm sending you the audio file now."

The phone clicked off. The new clue settled in the room, heavy and ominous. The lighthouse.

"You recognized that sound," Julia stated, her voice flat.

"It was part of my discredited evidence," he admitted, his voice rough with self-loathing.

The bitterness in his tone was so profound it cut through her anger. For the first time, Julia saw past her own sense of betrayal and truly glimpsed the depth of his professional ruin—the public humiliation he must have endured. He hadn't just lost a case; he had lost his career, his reputation. The sight of that old wound, still so raw, made her own grievances feel, for a moment, selfish.

He was standing so close now, the space between them charged with a decade of unspoken words and the raw energy of the storm. His gaze dropped to her lips, and the air grew thick, heavy with unspoken history. "Julia," he murmured, his voice husky with a decade of regret.

He leaned in, slow, deliberate, giving her every chance to pull away. She didn't. She couldn't. Her anger at him, her frustration, her deep-seated distrust—it was all there, a screaming chorus in her mind. But it was drowned out by a force far more elemental: the magnetic pull of this man, the ghost of the boy she had loved. She saw the question in his eyes, the same raw vulnerability she felt in her own chest. This wasn't just about desire. It was about seeing if anything, anything at all, was left to salvage from the wreckage of their past.

Her own eyes fluttered shut as his mouth came closer, a breath away from hers.

RRRING!

The sudden, shrill sound of a telephone shattered the moment. They sprang apart as if burned. On the corner of Alec's desk, an old, black landline was ringing, loud and insistent in the quiet office.

Alec stared at it, his face a mask of confusion and dread. "No one ever calls that line."

He crossed the room and snatched the receiver. "Hello?"

He listened, his brow furrowed. He held the phone out so Julia could hear. There was nothing but dead air. A dial tone. But then, underneath it, so faint she almost missed it, was another sound. A tinny, distorted echo.

It was the sound of their own voices.

"*...part of my discredited evidence... a tip came in about the lighthouse...*"

Julia's blood ran cold. The phone wasn't silent. It was playing their conversation back to them on a delay. Their sanctuary wasn't safe. It was bugged. Someone was listening. Someone had been listening to every single word.

Chapter 7: The Letters in the Attic

The tinny echo of their own voices died, leaving a silence in the room that was louder and more terrifying than the storm outside. The air crackled with paranoia.

Alec's reaction was explosive. With a low curse, he ripped the phone from the wall, smashing it against the floor. But his anger was cold, channeled into a frightening efficiency. "No more talking," he mouthed, his eyes hard. He immediately pulled his phone from his pocket, removed the battery, and gestured for her to do the same. He pointed to the notepad. *They heard everything. Assume they know where we'd go. Assume the house is watched.* His movements were swift, precise, and grimly professional. It was a jarring glimpse of the sharp, capable detective he used to be, a man who understood the rules of a very dangerous game.

While he tore apart his desk, Julia's training took over. She became methodical, her mind a grid of possibilities. She found the bug taped to the underside of a heavy drift-wood sculpture—a tiny black disc, no bigger than a dime. She held it up, and Alec crushed it between his fingers without a word.

She took the pen from him and wrote on the pad: *My attic. Sarah gave me a box.*

His eyes met hers, and a flicker of understanding, of renewed hope, passed between them. He nodded once.

Getting back to her house felt like navigating a mine-field. Inside, they moved in silence up the narrow, pull-down stairs to the attic. The air was hot, still, and thick with the smell of old wood, paper, and time itself. A single bare bulb cast a weak, yellow light, illuminating a city of forgotten things.

"The box is in the far corner," she whispered, the sound unnaturally loud in the quiet. "Behind the Christmas dec-orations."

They began the dusty work of excavation, moving heavy cartons in a silent, coordinated dance. As Alec shifted a large trunk, he uncovered a smaller, cedar-scented chest behind it. It wasn't the box she was looking for. This one was hers.

"What's this?" he murmured, his voice soft.

Julia's breath caught. She knew instantly. "Nothing. Just old things."

But he had already lifted the lid. Inside, nestled on a bed of faded velvet, was a collection of memories she had locked away. A photograph of the two of them, sixteen years old and awkward in formal wear at a school dance. A silly valentine he had made her in art class. A small, smooth piece of sea glass he'd given her for luck before a final exam. It was a time capsule of the relationship she had tried so hard to forget.

The air grew thick with unspoken words. The ghost in the attic was suddenly not Sarah's, but their own.

"I thought you would have thrown this stuff out," he said, his voice rough with an emotion she couldn't decipher.

"I'm a sentimental fool," she said, her attempt at a lighthearted tone falling flat. "And you're a packrat. We're even." She quickly closed the lid, shutting the ghosts back inside. "The box we're looking for is bigger. Cardboard."

The moment passed, but a new, fragile tension lingered between them. They finally unearthed it: a simple cardboard shoebox, the tape yellowed and brittle. They carried it to the center of the attic floor. With a sense of sacred reverence, Julia peeled away the tape. Inside, among ticket stubs and a dried corsage, was a thick bundle of letters, tied with a faded blue ribbon. Unsent.

They read them together, the only sound the soft crinkle of paper. The letters painted a horrifyingly clear picture. Sarah had been in a secret relationship with a boy she called 'C', a boy with a dark green luxury sedan and a silver ring.

"You lied to me, C," one letter read. *"You said it was just business, but the fish are dying. My dad's hauls are half what they used to be. This isn't just business, it's poison."*

Another was softer, more heartbreaking. *"I still re-member the boy who brought me wildflowers after my grandmother's funeral. I just don't know that boy anymore. Where did he go?"*

The last one, dated two days before the bonfire, was all cold fury. *"I have the real ledgers. I copied them from your father's desk. You think I'm stupid, but I'm not. Give me the money to get away from here, or I go to the press. I mean it, C. Ten thousand dollars."*

Julia read the last letter, her heart aching. A single tear traced a path through the dust on her cheek. She didn't notice it until Alec, without a word, pushed a clean mug and the thermos of coffee he must have grabbed on the way out of his office toward her across the floorboards. It was a simple, quiet gesture, but it felt profoundly kind. An acknowledgment of her pain. She gave him a small, grateful nod.

A soft thud from below announced Finn's arrival, summoned by a text from Julia. Grace was with him, her face etched with worry. Soon, the four of them were clustered under the bare bulb, a grim council of war.

"A blackmail plot," Alec said, his voice grim. "She was threatening to expose one of the town's elite."

"'C'," Finn mused, his laptop already open. "Could be Charles, Christopher, Connor... Clayton." He looked up, his eyes wide. "Clayton Ward?"

"His family car was a station wagon, and he couldn't afford a class ring, let alone one with a crest," Alec countered immediately. "It's not him."

"What about the Cranes?" Julia pressed. "They're the wealthiest family in town. The cannery was their business."

Grace sighed, a sound heavy with regret. "Mayor Crane's mother, Eleanora, came to my library a few days before Sarah vanished. She brought me tea in a thermos. We sat in my office, the door closed. She told me she considered me a pillar of the community, a sensible woman. Then she said she'd heard that poor, troubled Sarah Jenkins had been telling lies about a fine young man, a relative of hers. She said a girl like that, with her history, could ruin a boy's future with a single dramatic accusation. She looked at me, her eyes so full of sincere 'concern', and said, 'Friends help friends protect the community from... instability.' It was a threat, wrapped in a compliment." Grace's voice broke. "I was a coward. I let her flatter and frighten me into silence."

The detailed confession was chilling. It laid bare the insidious way the town's power structure operated.

"Okay, so it's likely a Crane," Finn said, typing furiously. "Mayor Evelyn has no sons. But her brother... Daniel Crane. He died about five years ago, but he had a son. Christopher."

"I remember him," Alec said, a dark look on his face. "He was a few years older. Wild. Got sent away to boarding school after a DUI. He was back in town that fall, the year Sarah disappeared."

"And according to this," Finn said, pointing to an old society page, "he was known for driving his father's dark green Jaguar. And look what he's wearing."

He zoomed in on the photo. On Christopher Crane's hand was a thick, silver ring, the crest unmistakable.

The four of them stared at the screen. The ghost finally had a name. Christopher Crane.

The quiet sense of victory, of a puzzle piece slamming into place, felt like the first clean breath Julia had taken in days. The warmth of the coffee, the focused energy of the team, the steady presence of Alec beside her—it was a fragile bubble of hope in the dark, suffocating night.

It was that feeling that made the end so brutal.

Drawn by a sudden noise from the street—a car door closing—Julia moved to the small, crescent-shaped window at the far end of the attic. She wiped a clean patch through the thick grime on the glass and peered down.

The rain had stopped. The street below was slick and black under the solitary streetlamp. And standing across the street, half-hidden in the shadow of a large oak tree, was a figure. Tall. Broad-shouldered. He wasn't just standing there. He was smoking, the red cherry of his cigarette glowing in the dark. He took a final, long drag and then flicked the butt into the street with a sharp, practiced motion that felt eerily familiar.

He knew they were in the attic. He was waiting.

Chapter 8: In Too Deep

The sight of the watcher—patient, menacing, and eerily familiar—shattered the fragile sense of progress they had built in the attic. The game had changed. They weren't just uncovering a secret; they were actively being hunted by someone who was always one step ahead.

"He knows we're here," Julia breathed, stepping back from the window, her heart hammering against her ribs.

Alec was instantly at her side, peering through the grimy glass. "We can't stay. We can't call the cops. We're on our own." His voice was grim, the detective in him assessing, planning. "Finn, create a diversion. Go out the front, make a lot of noise, drive away. Head north. Lead him off. Grace, you need to go home and lock your doors. Don't answer for anyone but us. Julia and I will go out the back."

It was a risky plan, but it was the only one they had. Ten minutes later, they heard Finn's car start up, his tires screeching as he peeled away from the curb. The shadowy figure across the street straightened up, flicked his cigarette, and melted back into the deeper darkness, following the sound.

"Now," Alec said, grabbing Julia's arm.

They slipped out the back door into the pre-dawn chill, the air thick with the smell of wet earth and the coming sea mist. They didn't have a clear destination, only a new, terrifying name: Christopher Crane. They also had a clue, a line from Sarah's last, desperate letter, which Alec had shown her on his phone.

"I'm taking the ledgers to our place. The real ones. Where the sky meets the sea. They'll be safe there until I can use them."

"'Our place'," Julia whispered as they navigated the dark backyards. A jolt of recognition, cold and sharp, went through her. She knew exactly where Sarah meant. A secluded, treacherous cove north of town, accessible only by a dangerous cliffside path. A place where the sky truly did seem to meet the sea.

The trek to the cove at dawn was a journey into a grey, misty purgatory. The path was barely a path anymore, just a muddy, eroded scar on the cliff face.

"Slow down," Alec cautioned, his voice tight as he grabbed her arm to steady her on a particularly narrow ledge.

"We don't have time to slow down," she snapped, pulling away. "He could be right behind us."

"And a misstep here is a fall you don't walk away from," he shot back, his frustration boiling over. "For once in your life, can you please stop and think instead of just charging forward?"

"Oh, that's brilliant coming from you!" she retorted, spinning to face him. "The man who is so afraid of making a mistake that he'd rather let a murderer walk free than take a real risk! You're not cautious, Alec. You're paralyzed."

"And you're reckless!" he roared. "I was the one who had to tell Sarah's parents there was nothing more I could do! I won't have to do the same for your mother."

His words should have hurt, but instead, they clarified everything. "You think I'm reckless," she said, her voice shaking but clear, "but I'm just not willing to let another ten years go by in silence. That silence is what killed her, Alec. Not a fall from a cliff."

Before he could answer, the ground beneath her feet shifted with a low, sickening groan. A web of cracks appeared in the muddy path.

"Julia, move!" Alec yelled.

But it was too late. With a sound like tearing fabric, the section of the cliff face where she stood gave way. She cried out as the ground fell away, a landslide of mud and rock pulling her down.

In a flash, Alec lunged, throwing his body flat against the stable part of the path. He caught her wrist, his grip like a steel manacle, just as her feet went over the edge. She dangled there, the sea churning a hundred feet below.

"Don't let go!" she screamed.

"Never," he grunted, his face contorted with effort. With a surge of pure, desperate strength, he hauled her upward, scraping her body against the raw cliffside until she could get her footing and scramble back onto the solid path.

They collapsed together, trembling and gasping. He didn't let her go. He held her, his arms wrapped around her, his face buried in her hair. She clung to him, her face pressed against the rough, damp wool of his jacket, inhaling the scent of rain and wet earth and him. It wasn't just his strength that she felt, but the fine, uncontrollable tremor in his hands as he held her. It was the ragged sound of his breathing in her ear, not just from exertion, but from sheer, unadulterated fear. And in that moment, she understood. His anger, his overbearing caution, his frustration—it wasn't about the past. Not entirely. It was about his profound, terrifying fear of losing her, too.

After a long moment, they pulled apart, shaken but resolute. They found the gnarled cypress tree that marked the spot. Buried near its roots was a small, steel, waterproof box. Alec pried it open with his knife.

Inside, nestled on a bed of what had once been cotton, was a slim notebook, a few loose photographs, and a roll of undeveloped film. And sitting on top of the notebook was a single, perfectly pressed wildflower—a blue lupine, just like the ones that grew near the cliffs. Just like the ones Sarah had mentioned in her letter. It was a fragile, tragic reminder of the girl she had been, and the love she had thought was real. Julia gently set it aside, her heart aching.

The notebook was Sarah's ledger, a meticulous record of the cannery's crimes. One photo showed a smug Christopher Crane. Another showed him in a quiet, intense conversation with a uniformed, much younger Clayton Ward.

Julia's hands trembled as she picked up the last photograph. It was of Sarah, smiling, but her eyes looked haunted. It was stuck to another photo behind it. She carefully peeled them apart. On the back of Sarah's picture, a single, terrifying phrase was scrawled in her handwriting: *He knows I have this.*

But it was the front of the hidden photo that made Julia's blood run cold. It was a blurry, candid shot of the dark green Jaguar, parked on a dirt road. It was focused on the driver's side door, and on the silver handle, clearly visible, was a dark, brownish-red smear.

The unmistakable trace of a bloody handprint.

Chapter 9: Whispers and Wounds

The bloody handprint on the photograph seemed to burn in the cool, misty air of the cliffs. It was a silent scream from the past, a definitive, horrifying testament to violence. All the whispers, threats, and half-remembered clues had finally coalesced into this one grisly image. Sarah hadn't just disappeared. She had fought for her life.

Alec stared at the photo, his face a grim, stony mask, but Julia could see the fury in the tight set of his jaw. The raw terror of the landslide had been replaced by a cold, clarifying rage.

"This changes everything," she said, her voice quiet but steady. "This is proof."

"It's proof we can't take to the police," he countered, gesturing to the other photo—the one of a young Clayton Ward in quiet conversation with Christopher Crane. "Ward is part of it. He has been from the beginning."

They were truly alone now, adrift on a sea of conspiracy with no safe harbor in sight. The roll of undeveloped film in the box felt heavy with possibility, a ghost waiting for the light.

"We need to get this film developed," Julia said. "Somewhere far from here. And we need to talk to the one person Ward had to silence personally. The one person who saw that car."

"Ruby Santiago," Alec finished, his eyes meeting hers. A new, unspoken understanding passed between them. The arguments were done. They were a team now, bound by the terrible knowledge of what they held in their hands.

It was late afternoon by the time they reached Ruby's small, overstuffed house on the edge of town. The parlor window was a magpie's nest of porcelain figurines and stacks of old magazines. Ruby cracked the door open, her face draining of color when she saw them.

"I can't talk to you," she said, trying to push the door closed. "You saw what happened at the meeting. I've said too much."

"We know you were threatened, Ruby," Julia said, placing her hand on the door. "We know who threatened you. Please. We just need you to tell us the truth."

Hesitantly, Ruby let them in. The air inside was cloying, thick with the scent of potpourri and old secrets. She led them to her cluttered parlor. On her mantelpiece, among the porcelain figurines and dusty silk flowers, was a beautiful, intricate ship in a bottle. A perfect, tiny vessel with its sails unfurled, forever trapped just inches from a painted blue sea. The sight was strangely poignant.

"You don't know what you're doing," Ruby whispered, wringing her hands. "You're stirring up things that can't be put back."

Julia didn't waste time. She laid the photograph of the bloody handprint on the coffee table. Ruby gasped, her hand flying to her mouth, a choked sob escaping her lips.

"That's the car," she breathed, tears welling. "That's the one I saw."

Her story came out in a torrent of fear and guilt. "I told the officer at the desk what I saw. The next day, Clayton Ward came here. He sat right where you're sitting. He told me I was mistaken. That I'd been drinking. He said a murder investigation was serious business, and false statements could have... consequences. For me. For my son."

"He made me feel crazy," Ruby sobbed. "Small and stupid and crazy."

"I'm so sorry, Ruby," Julia said, her own voice thick with a sudden, sharp guilt. "I was a kid, wrapped up in my own world. I heard the whispers... that you were just a gossip. And I never questioned them. I was wrong."

Ruby looked at her, a flicker of surprise in her tear-filled eyes.

Hearing the story seemed to break something in Alec. He sank back into his chair. "I was there," he said, his voice hollow. "I was at the station when Ruby's retraction came in. My gut told me her original statement was good. But Clayton... he was my partner. My friend. He told me I was letting my personal connection to you and Sarah cloud my judgment." Alec looked at Julia, his eyes filled with a profound, soul-deep shame. "I let him convince me. I trusted him over my own instincts. I failed her."

"You didn't know," she said softly. "He was your friend. How could you have known?"

As she said the words, she realized they were true. In that moment, looking at the profound, decades-old shame on his face, the anger she had nursed for ten years didn't just fade; it felt hollow, pointless. He hadn't abandoned her back then. He had been drowning right beside her, and she had been too lost in her own grief to see it. The realization was a painful, clarifying light.

The shared confessions created a strange, solemn intimacy in the cluttered room. They were three broken pieces of the same tragedy.

"Christopher Crane was the one in the car," Julia said, pulling them back to the facts. "But he's dead. So who are we up against now?"

"The person who threatened me," Ruby whispered. "Clayton Ward. And whoever he's protecting." A flicker of memory crossed her face. "I saw Christopher there once," she said, her eyes distant. "Down by the boathouse, wrestling with a brand new, heavy brass padlock. I remember thinking it was so strange... like putting a diamond collar on a stray dog. A lock that expensive didn't belong on a rotting old door. He saw me watching and gave me a look that turned my blood to ice."

The boathouse again. A hidden, locked room inside a derelict building. It had to be the final puzzle piece.

"Thank you, Ruby," Julia said, a new sense of purpose surging through her. "You've been incredibly brave."

As she stood to leave, a cheerful electronic chime sounded in the room. Ruby's phone, sitting on the end table beside her. Ruby glanced at the screen, and a look of pure, animal terror washed over her face. Her hand started to shake so violently the phone clattered against the table.

"What is it?" Alec asked, instantly on alert.

Wordlessly, Ruby picked up the phone and turned the screen toward them.

It was a text message from an unknown number. It contained no words.

It was just a photograph. A crystal-clear picture of her own front door, taken from across the street. And standing in the foreground, partially obscuring the view, was the sleeve of a man's jacket and a hand, casually flicking a cigarette into the gutter.

The threat wasn't coming. It was already there. It was right outside.

Chapter 10: Break-in at the Boathouse

The photograph on Ruby's phone was a declaration of war. The watcher wasn't just a ghost anymore; he was a tangible presence, a man with a phone and a camera, marking them, toying with them. The casual, arrogant flick of the cigarette in the photo was a signature, a taunt. He was telling them he was there.

Ruby let out a choked, terrified whimper. Panic seized the cluttered parlor.

"Get away from the windows," Alec commanded, his voice a low, urgent growl that cut through the fear. He was already moving, every trace of the vulnerable man from moments before gone, replaced by the grimly efficient protector. He peered through a gap in the curtains. "The street's empty. He's gone. He just wanted us to know."

"He wanted *me* to know," Ruby cried, wrapping her arms around herself. "He's telling me what happens if I talk."

The message had put a target on her back. Julia felt a surge of guilt and a fresh wave of cold fury. They had brought this danger to Ruby's door. Now they had to end it.

"The boathouse," Julia said, her eyes meeting Alec's across the room. "The closet Ruby saw. It has to be tonight. Now. Before he has time to clear it out."

"It's a trap, Julia," Alec argued, his voice low. "He's expecting us to do something reckless."

"He's right," she agreed. "And we're going to do it anyway. We have no other move, Alec. We are out of time."

His jaw was tight, but he saw the truth in her eyes. He gave a single, sharp nod.

The dead of night found them once again at the edge of the cove, the abandoned boathouse a hulking shape against a moonless sky. The air was unnaturally still, the eerie quiet a stark contrast to the storm that had raged just twenty-four hours earlier. This time, there was no fumbling with lock picks. Alec had brought a small toolkit from his truck, and in his hand, he carried the crowbar the watcher had left behind during their first encounter. With a single, powerful wrench, the wood splintered and the door swung open with a low groan.

They slipped inside. Following Ruby's directions, they found the small storage closet at the back, secured with the heavy brass padlock. On the third try with the crowbar, the hasp tore away from the dry-rotted wood with a sharp crack, and the door swung inward.

The closet was small and damp. It contained a few old cans of paint and a single metal filing box. Julia lifted the box and placed it on the floor. She pried it open with the tip of a screwdriver. Inside, resting on top of a thick file folder, was a tarnished silver flask, monogrammed with a single, ornate 'C'. The air suddenly smelled faintly of old, expensive whiskey. Beneath it was the file.

The label on the tab was stark: *MCPD – Active Payments.* It was a meticulous record of payments from the Crane Cannery's parent corporation to a single recipient: Clayton Ward.

"We've got him," she breathed, a triumphant, dizzying relief washing over her. "We've finally got him."

"Got who?"

The voice, calm and laced with a cold amusement, came from the main doorway. Clayton Ward stood there, silhouetted against the faint light from the cove, his gun pointed directly at them.

"Really, Alec? I taught you better than this," Clayton said, taking a slow step into the boathouse. "Returning to the scene of the crime? It's a rookie mistake."

"It all makes sense now, Clay," Alec said, slowly getting to his feet, positioning himself between Julia and the gun. "The money. Was it worth it? Was it worth her life?"

Clayton chuckled, a dry, humorless sound. "Sarah was a loose end," he said with a shrug. "A sentimental girl who cried about her worthless boyfriend right up to the end. Pathetic. She made a stupid choice, and I just cleaned it up." He gestured with the gun. "Now, be a good friend and slide that file over."

"It's over," Julia said, her voice shaking but defiant as she clutched the file.

In that split second, Alec moved. He dove to the side, grabbing a heavy, splintered boat oar and swinging it low, knocking a stack of paint cans into Clayton's path. Clayton stumbled, firing a shot that went wide, the explosion of the gunshot deafening in the enclosed space.

Chaos erupted. Alec engaged his old friend in a brutal, desperate fight. He ducked under a wild swing from Clayton, using their old police academy training against him, and drove his knee hard into Clayton's side. Clayton grunted, his friendship forgotten in a mask of rage, and brought the butt of his pistol down on Alec's shoulder. Alec staggered back, pain shooting down his arm, but he came back swinging, landing a solid right cross that sent Clayton stumbling. Julia, seeing her chance, grabbed the heavy silver flask and hurled it at Clayton's head, making him cry out and giving Alec the opening he needed. He drove his shoulder into Clayton's chest, sending them both crashing into a stack of old wooden crates. Clayton's head hit the wall with a sickening crack, and he slumped to the ground, momentarily dazed.

"Go!" Alec yelled, grabbing the file from Julia's hands. "Run!"

They scrambled for the door, but just as they reached it, he grabbed her arm, spinning her around to face him. The air was electric with adrenaline and fear and something more.

"Julia," he said, his voice raw.

And then his mouth was on hers. It wasn't a gentle kiss. It was desperate, fierce, a primal claiming in the heart of the storm. And as he kissed her, a stunning, silent clarity cut through Julia's fear. This wasn't just about desperation or adrenaline. It was an answer. A defiant roar against the sirens and the flames. In the center of the violence, she found the only quiet, solid thing in the world: him.

The piercing wail of distant sirens shattered the moment.

They broke apart, their eyes wide. Backup. Clayton had called for backup.

"He was never going to let us walk out of here," Alec said, his voice grim as he pulled her toward the door.

They burst out into the night and ran, not looking back. But as they reached the tree line, a sudden, bright orange glow illuminated the cove behind them. Julia turned. Flames were licking up the side of the old boathouse, voracious and fast.

He was destroying the evidence. All of it.

They ran on, the sound of the approaching sirens growing louder, the roar of the fire at their backs, the ghosts of Misty Cove finally, truly, set ablaze.

Chapter 11:
Scorched Earth

Dawn broke not with light, but with smoke. From the small window of Finn's apartment above his bar, The Salty Dog, Julia could see a thick, grey-black plume rising over the cove. The boathouse, the epicenter of their discoveries, was gone. All that remained was a smoking pyre, its ashes mingling with the morning mist.

The adrenaline from the night had long since bled away, leaving behind a deep, shaking exhaustion and the bitter taste of defeat. They had escaped, but it didn't feel like a victory. It felt like they had been routed, their every move anticipated and countered, their one tangible victory—the file—feeling small and insignificant against the inferno.

Alec sat in a worn armchair, a glass of whiskey untouched in his hand, his gaze fixed on the rising smoke. His shoulder, bruised and swollen where Clayton's pistol had struck him, was a dark testament to the night's violence. The desperate, searing kiss they had shared now hung in the air between them, a ghost as real as the ones they were chasing. It was a question with no easy answer, a moment of impossible connection forged in chaos, and neither of them knew what to do with it.

Guilt was a physical presence in the room, thick and suffocating. Alec's guilt was for fighting his friend, for leading them into a trap, for failing to protect them. Julia's was for the ever-expanding circle of danger she had drawn around the people she cared about—her mother, Grace, Finn, and especially Ruby, who was now a marked woman.

Finn, ever the loyal soldier, moved between them like a battlefield medic, his usual buoyant energy replaced by a quiet, grim focus. He had a first-aid kit open on the coffee table.

"Let me see that," he said to Julia, gently tilting her chin to inspect a raw scrape on her cheek. He cleaned it with an antiseptic wipe, his touch careful. "The official story is already making the rounds. Mayor Crane held a press conference an hour ago. Called it a 'tragic case of arson, likely perpetrated by outside agitators seeking to sow discord in our peaceful community'."

"Outside agitators," Julia repeated, the words a bitter pill. "She means me."

"She means both of you," Finn said, his eyes flicking to Alec. "Clayton is the hero. He apparently responded to a suspected break-in and was 'assaulted' before the perpetrators set the fire to cover their tracks."

It was a perfect, airtight narrative. They had been completely outmaneuvered.

As Finn worked, Julia spread the recovered file across the coffee table. The paper was damp and slightly torn from the chaotic fight, but the contents were legible. It was damning, but Alec had been right. It was a collection of financial records. Clayton could create a dozen plausible lies. Their investigation hadn't just stalled; it had hit a brick wall.

"So what do we do?" Julia demanded, her frustration mounting. "We just give up? Let him win?"

"I don't know!" Alec's voice rose, raw with exhaustion and fear. "All I know is that last night he tried to kill us. He would have shot us and left us in that fire, and Crane would have given him a medal for it. We are in over our heads."

"So you *are* giving up," she accused, her own fear manifesting as anger. "Just like last time. As soon as it gets too hard, too dangerous, you retreat."

"Holding back?" He stood up, his eyes blazing with a pain so deep it shocked her. "I am trying to keep you alive! What more do you want from me?"

"I want the man who kissed me last night!" she cried, the words torn from her, raw and reckless. "The man who fought for me. Where is he? Or was that just part of the act, too? A moment of weakness before you retreated back inside your walls?"

The hurt that flashed across his face was so profound it made her wish she could snatch the words back from the air. Before he could answer, Finn cleared his throat, holding a small stack of mail. "I, uh, swung by your mom's house on the way here. Figured you'd want this."

Julia took the mail, shuffling through it distractedly. She saw a plain manila envelope with no postage and no return address. It must have been slipped through the mail slot. Her fingers felt numb as she tore it open.

Inside wasn't a note. It was a drawing. A charcoal sketch, rendered with an unnervingly skillful hand. It was a picture of her and Alec, from the night before, huddled together in the boathouse just before the fight. It captured the intimacy of the moment, the way he was protectively shielding her. As she looked closer, a wave of nausea rolled through her. She recognized the paper. It was torn from a sketchbook, slightly yellowed with age, with a distinctive watermark in the corner. It was a page from one of Sarah's old sketchbooks. The killer hadn't just watched them; they had kept a trophy for ten years and were now using it to defile a new memory.

Scrawled across the bottom in stark, red letters was a single word.

STOP.

She showed it to Alec. He stared at the sketch, and every last bit of color drained from his face. The fight went out of him, replaced by a cold, hollow dread. This was the proof he needed, but not the kind he wanted. It was proof that his worst fears were real.

He looked at Julia, his expression shuttered and distant. The man who had kissed her with such desperate passion just hours before was gone, replaced by a stranger.

"I can't," he said, his voice barely a whisper. "I can't do this."

"Alec, don't," she pleaded, seeing where this was going.

"I came back to this case to find justice for Sarah," he said, his voice flat and devoid of emotion. "But all I've done is lead you into the line of fire. I watched one Hart girl get destroyed by this town. I will not be responsible for another."

He turned and walked toward the door, his movements stiff, his shoulders slumped with the weight of his decision.

"Alec, please," she begged, her voice breaking. "Don't do this. Don't leave me."

His hand rested on the doorknob, his knuckles white. For a long second, his entire body seemed frozen in an agony of indecision, his shoulders tense with the effort of not turning around. Then, he forced himself to twist the knob. "This is the only way I can protect you," he said, his voice thick with unshed tears. "From them. And from me."

And with that, he opened the door and walked out, leaving her alone with the ashes of their investigation, a damning file she couldn't use, and a terrifying sketch that proved the killer was not just watching her, but seeing right into her heart.

Chapter 12: Mask Off

The silence Alec left behind was a physical weight. For an hour after he walked out the door, Julia didn't move. She just sat there, in the quiet of Finn's apartment, the damning sketch on the table in front of her, feeling the full, crushing force of her isolation. He was gone.

But beneath the grief, a different feeling began to smolder. A hard, cold anger. They had done this. The people who killed Sarah, who had terrorized this town for a decade, had finally succeeded in tearing her and Alec apart. They expected her to retreat. They didn't know her very well.

Her despair began to calcify, hardening into a diamond-sharp resolve. Finn watched her, his expression full of concern. "Jules, what are you thinking?"

"I'm thinking I'm done hiding," she said, her voice devoid of its earlier tremor. "I'm going to see the Chief of Police."

"What? No!" Finn protested. "That's insane! He tried to kill you!"

"I know," she said, her eyes like chips of ice. "And I'm going to watch his mask slip."

The Misty Cove Police Station was sterile and quiet. Julia walked past the front desk without stopping and pushed open the door to Clayton Ward's office without knocking.

He was on the phone, laughing. He hung up when he saw her. "Well, look what the tide dragged in. To what do I owe the displeasure, Julia? Come to confess to arson?"

"I came to show you something," she said, closing the door. She slid a single piece of paper from the file across his desk. "This is just one statement, Clayton," she said, her voice dangerously calm. "A little appetizer. The full file from the boathouse is very... thorough. And my editors have a copy in a very safe place."

Clayton glanced at it, his expression of bored amusement not changing, but she saw a flicker of something in his eyes. "You're playing with fire, Julia. You come into my town, stir up trouble, get a girl like Ruby Santiago all worked up, and then you burn down a historic landmark."

"Was Christopher Crane a 'good friend'?" she pressed. "Or just a good paycheck?"

The mention of the name made him flinch. He stood up, leaning his knuckles on the desk. "You have no idea what you're messing with. This is bigger than some dead girl."

As he spoke, he reached for a pack of cigarettes on his desk. He tapped one out and lit it, then with a sharp, practiced motion, he flicked the spent match into an ashtray. It was the same motion she had seen from the attic window. The watcher. A cold dread washed over her.

The office door opened, and Mayor Crane swept in. "Clayton, what is she doing here? I thought we agreed—" She stopped short when she saw Julia. "Get her out of here."

"She's making accusations," Clayton said, a smug look returning to his face. "Wild ones."

They stood there together, about to close in on her, when the door opened again.

Alec stood in the doorway. He looked tired, haggard, but his presence filled the room. A wave of relief so intense it almost buckled her knees washed over Julia, followed immediately by a hot flush of anger. *How did he know to be here?* The thought was both comforting and infuriating. He had left her, but he hadn't abandoned her. He was watching her, and she didn't know whether to feel grateful or suffocated.

Clayton turned his attention to Alec, a look of genuine disappointment mixed with his sneer. "Always rushing in to save a Hart. Some things never change, do they, partner? Remember pulling her out of that car wreck after the prom? You were a real hero then, too. Look how well that turned out for everyone."

The cruel, twisted memory hung in the air, a testament to their dead friendship.

"Her lawyer is on his way down from the city," Alec said, his voice flat and dangerous, the lie smooth and utterly convincing. "I'd imagine he'll have a lot of questions about witness intimidation and the chain of custody for evidence in a ten-year-old homicide case."

Clayton looked like he was about to call the bluff, his hand inching toward his weapon. But Mayor Crane placed a perfectly manicured hand on his arm, a silent command. Her cold eyes assessed the situation, calculating the political risk. "Let her go, Chief," she said, her voice soft but laced with steel. "For now." The message was clear: she was making the decision, and this was a strategic retreat, not a surrender.

Alec still wouldn't look at Julia, but as he stepped aside to let her pass, he spoke in a whisper so low only she could hear. "It's not just about the cannery. Ask them about the shoreline development deal."

He had given her a new thread. He was gone, but he wasn't out.

Julia walked out of the station, her head held high. She made it to her rental car in the parking lot, her hands shaking as she fumbled for her keys.

"Hart."

She turned. Clayton was standing right behind her, his friendly mask completely gone, his eyes cold and dead.

"This is your last warning," he said, his voice a venomous whisper. "You're a reporter. You know how these things go. Tragic accidents happen all the time. Your mother... she still lives in that old house, right? Be a shame if something happened. Faulty wiring. A gas leak."

He smiled, a chilling, predatory expression. "Stop. Or I will burn everything you love to the ground."

He turned and walked back into the station, leaving her standing alone in the sterile morning light, the threat hanging in the air like poison. He had threatened her family. The betrayal was no longer a matter of law or justice. It was personal. It was a blood debt.

Chapter 13: Storm Shelter

The tires of Julia's rental car slid on the wet asphalt as she drove, the world outside a blur of wind and rain. A new storm had descended upon Misty Cove, a furious tempest that mirrored the maelstrom in her soul. Clayton's threat echoed in her mind, a poison seeping into every thought. *I will burn everything you love to the ground.* He had threatened her mother. The thought was a physical pain, a cold, hard knot of terror in her chest.

She couldn't go home. She couldn't go to Finn's. There was only one place left, one person she trusted without question.

She pulled up to Grace's cottage. The lights were on, a warm, welcoming glow against the violent storm. Grace opened the door before she knocked, her face a mixture of worry and grim resolve. "I was hoping you wouldn't come," she said, pulling Julia into the warm, book-scented air. "And I knew you would. It's not safe for you in the house."

"I didn't know where else to go," Julia admitted, her voice trembling.

"I know, child." Grace led her not to the living room, but through the kitchen to a heavy wooden door set low in the wall. "Your mother is safe. I called her an hour ago and told her she had a gas leak and needed to come stay with my sister in the next town over. She's on her way there now."

The relief that washed over Julia was so profound it almost buckled her knees. "Grace, thank you."

"We protect our own," Grace said, opening the door to a set of steep, stone steps. "This is the only place I can guarantee they won't be listening."

The root cellar was small and cool, the air thick with the earthy smell of damp soil and old preserves. It was claustrophobic, but it felt like a sanctuary. Julia had been down there for less than ten minutes when the cellar door opened again. A figure descended the stone steps, rain dripping from his jacket. Alec.

He stopped at the bottom of the stairs, the space suddenly feeling impossibly small. "How did you know?" she asked, her voice barely a whisper.

"Where else would you go?" he answered, his voice rough. "I had to make sure you were safe."

The cellar door opened a third time. Grace stood at the top of the stairs, holding a dusty, tape-sealed box. "I think it's time for this," she said, her voice heavy. "Sarah's mother gave it to me the week after the funeral. She showed up on my doorstep in the rain, holding this box like it was made of glass. Her eyes were hollowed out. She just said, 'I can't have her ghost in my house anymore, Grace. You keep her safe for me.' And I have."

She handed the box to Julia and quietly closed the door, leaving them alone again, this time with the final effects of their ghost.

They opened the box together. Inside were things that made Julia's heart ache: a diary, a half-finished sketch, a mixtape. And at the very bottom, tucked inside a hollowed-out copy of *Wuthering Heights*, was a single, sealed envelope addressed to the District Attorney.

Julia's hands trembled as she opened it. The paper was thin, almost translucent with age. The ink was a faded blue, and in one spot, next to Clayton's name, was a tiny, circular smudge, as if a single teardrop had fallen there and dried long ago. It was a physical remnant of Sarah's fear.

They read it together, their heads bent close in the warm lamplight, the storm raging above them. The letter was a clear, concise, and damning account of everything. It named Christopher Crane as her lover and Clayton Ward as his threatening accomplice.

Reading the words, seeing the final, irrefutable proof, broke down the last of their defenses.

"I'm so sorry, Julia," Alec said, his voice thick with emotion. He finally looked at her, his eyes full of the torment he had tried to hide. "I left because I thought I was protecting you. I saw what happened to her, and every time I look at you, I see you at the edge of that same cliff. The thought of you falling... it's the only thing that truly scares me."

"I know," she said, her own tears falling freely now. Her voice gained a new strength. "So stop trying to protect me from the fall. Trust me to be your partner instead. We face this together, Alec. All of it. No more running, not from them, and not from this." She squeezed his hand. "Together."

"Together," he repeated, his voice full of relief and resolve. He reached out, his thumb gently wiping a tear from her cheek. It was a quiet, deliberate joining, a moment of peace found in the most unlikely of places. He pulled her closer, and she leaned her head against his good shoulder, the two of them finding shelter not just from the tempest outside, but from the ones within.

After a long while, Julia picked up the letter again, needing to arm herself with Sarah's final words. Her eyes fell upon the last paragraph, a section she had skimmed over in her initial emotional haze.

"...I know this is bigger than just Christopher and his father. Clayton isn't smart enough to orchestrate this. He's muscle. There's someone else, someone pulling the strings. The one I'm truly afraid of. The one who watches, who cleans up the messes. He's the one who promised me, through Clayton, that he would 'burn everything I love to the ground' if I spoke a word of this..."

Julia's breath hitched. She looked up at Alec, her eyes wide. "Alec..."

He saw the look on her face and immediately understood. "In the parking lot," he said, his voice a horrified whisper. "That's what Clayton said to you. That exact phrase."

It hit them at the same time. A chilling, perfect echo across a decade. Clayton hadn't been making his own threat. He had been delivering a message. He was quoting his boss.

Christopher was dead. Clayton was the enforcer. But the true mastermind, the man who had architected this whole conspiracy, was still out there. And he was very much alive.

Chapter 14: The Unraveling

The revelation in the root cellar changed the air between them. The separate, jagged pieces of their investigation had finally slammed together to form a single, terrifying picture. There was a mastermind, a ghost pulling the strings for over a decade.

"The shoreline development deal," Julia said, the words Alec had whispered to her in the police station now burning with significance. "It was never just about covering up a murder. It's about money."

"Generational wealth," Alec agreed, his face grim. "The kind people kill to protect." He was a detective again, his mind sharp, focused, and angry. "We need proof."

Back in Grace's kitchen, they formulated a frantic, desperate plan. Finn, on a secure video call, was their digital operative, tasked with digging into the development deal.

Julia would go to her mother to uncover the truth of the Hart family's history with the Cranes. And Alec would handle the Town Hall.

"I'm going to the archives, the planning office," he said. "Somewhere in that building is a paper trail that isn't public. I have to find it." His eyes met hers, full of a fierce resolve. "We do this together, remember? This is my part."

The moment they stepped out of Grace's cottage, the fragile sense of safety shattered. A dark, heavy-duty truck, the kind used by the cannery's maintenance crew, with the faded Crane logo still visible on the door, peeled out from a side street and hurtled directly toward them.

"Julia, get in!" Alec yelled, shoving her toward his own truck and diving into the driver's seat.

He slammed the truck in reverse, tires screaming, just as the cannery truck would have crushed them. What followed was a brutal, terrifying chase through the rain-slicked, winding streets of Misty Cove. Their pursuer was relentless, ramming their bumper, trying to force them off the road. On a sharp turn near the old cannery, Alec spun the wheel hard, sending their truck into a controlled skid. Their pursuer couldn't correct in time and plowed straight into a row of heavy shipping pallets, the sound of crunching metal echoing through the dusk.

"Go!" Alec yelled, pushing her out the passenger door. "Get to your mother. I'll handle the Town Hall. Go now!"

He sprinted off into the labyrinth of warehouses, leaving Julia to steal away on foot.

An hour later, soaked and shaken, Julia arrived at her aunt's house. She found her mother in the kitchen. "I need you to tell me about Grandpa's business," she said. "The one he had with Alec's grandfather."

Her mother stiffened, a flicker of an old, deep pain in her eyes. Finally, the truth spilled out. Their grandfathers had trusted a third, silent partner to handle a lucrative land deal for the entire northern shoreline: Richard Crane.

"He cheated them," her mother said, her voice choked with sorrow. "He used their money to buy the land for a secret trust in his own family's name, then cooked the books to make it look like their business had gone bankrupt. He was never the same after that, Julia. He walked around like a ghost in his own house. That kind of betrayal, from a man he called a friend... it doesn't just steal your money. It hollows a person out from the inside."

At that same moment, Alec was inside the Town Hall. He had slipped in through a maintenance door. He found Mayor Crane's office at the end of the hall. The door was locked, as he expected. He pulled a slim tension wrench and a single pick from a hidden seam in his wallet—a skill he hadn't used in years but had learned from a seasoned burglar during his rookie days. The silence of the hallway was absolute, broken only by the faint, metallic click of the tumblers. After a tense thirty seconds, the lock gave way with a soft snick.

He bypassed her desk, heading for the large credenza against the wall. He found the blueprints, the contracts. And tucked away at the very back, in a folder marked *Private*, he found the original charter for the secret trust. The sole, primary beneficiary and controlling trustee was no longer a board. It was a single person. Mayor Evelyn Crane.

A text from Finn vibrated in his pocket, confirming it all. *IT'S ALL HER. SHE'S NOT PROTECTING HER FATHER'S LEGACY. SHE'S PROTECTING HER OWN PAYDAY.*

He heard a floorboard creak behind him. He spun around, but it was too late.

The door burst open. Clayton Ward stood there, flanked by two deputies. The fight was short, brutal, and hopeless. They overwhelmed him, slamming him against the wall, wrenching his arms behind his back.

Clayton stepped forward, a cruel, triumphant smile on his face as he picked up the trust document. "Looking for something, partner?" he sneered. He leaned in close, his voice a low, triumphant whisper. "Don't you worry about Julia. Now that you're out of the way, we'll be sure to take *real* good care of her."

He nodded to the deputies. "Get him out of here. He's been charged with breaking and entering, assault, and arson. Looks like he's finally going away for a long, long time."

As they dragged a bruised and struggling Alec from the office, his heart sank. He had the truth, but it was useless. He was caught. And Julia, wherever she was, was still out there, completely, terrifyingly alone.

Chapter 15: On the Edge

The hours after the chase bled into a long, terrifying silence. Julia had found refuge in a cheap, anonymous motel a town away, the garish neon sign outside casting a sickly glow into her room. She had tried Alec's phone a dozen times. Each call went straight to voicemail, his familiar, steady greeting a torturous echo from a world that no longer existed. She tried Finn. No answer. Grace. Nothing.

She was an island, completely cut off. The silence was a crushing weight, filled with the ghosts of her worst fears. Alec was gone. Clayton had him. The threat against her mother was a cold knot of dread in her stomach. Every step forward had only led them deeper into the darkness, and now, she was lost in it, alone.

Sleep was impossible. The only thing she could think to do was move. Before midnight, she was back in her car, driving without a destination, letting the winding coastal highway pull her forward. On instinct, she took the turn-off for the old Point Reyes lighthouse road.

She parked and walked the rest of the way. The lighthouse stood on the edge of the world, a skeletal white tower against a starless sky. The wind, a constant, battering force, howled around the crumbling structure. Julia leaned against the cold iron railing, the wind tearing at her hair, and stared at the violent, black sea below.

The memory of the root cellar ambushed her, not as a thought, but as a physical sensation. She could almost feel the rough wool of Alec's jacket against her cheek, the solid warmth of his shoulder beneath her head. She could hear his voice, thick with a decade of pain, confessing his fear of losing her. *'It's the only thing that truly scares me.'* The memory wasn't a comfort; it was a clarifying fire. He had pushed her away not out of weakness, but out of a fierce, misguided love. Forgiveness wasn't just about letting go of the past. It was about trusting in the future. A future she was now terrified she had destroyed for both of them.

A pair of headlights appeared on the road behind her. It was Finn. He got out, his face pale and grim in the moonlight.

"I figured you'd end up somewhere like this," he said. "Poetic and depressing. It's your brand."

"Finn, what's happening? I can't reach anyone."

"I know. I had to ditch my phone. They're tracking us." He handed her a steaming cup of coffee from a thermos. "It's bad, Jules. The news is saying Alec was arrested for the boathouse fire. They're painting him as an unstable ex-cop obsessed with you."

The words were like a physical blow. They were burying him, just like they had buried Sarah.

"I've hit a wall," Finn said, showing her his tablet. The screen was filled with the seemingly random annotations from Sarah's ledger. "It's not any cipher I recognize. It's just... numbers."

Julia stared at the screen, at the jumble of figures. Then her eyes flicked to the small, embedded map of Misty Cove on Finn's program. An idea sparked. "They're not a code to be cracked, Finn," she said slowly, her own excitement building. "They're coordinates. Pull up the full navigational chart."

Finn's eyes widened as he typed. A moment later, red pins began to dot the map of the cove. "You're a genius," he breathed. "They're GPS coordinates. The dump sites. Every last one." He zoomed in. "But there's one last set, set apart from the others. It's not in the water. It's a location on land." The final red pin was blinking on the stretch of cliffs just south of where they were standing.

This was it. The final piece of the puzzle. In that moment, staring at the blinking red light, something inside Julia shifted. The despair and fear burned away, forged by the wind and the grief into something new. Something hard, cold, and unbreakable. Resolve.

"Okay," she said, her voice steady now, clear and sharp as glass. "Here's what we're going to do. We can't go to the police. We have to force a confession, and we have to do it where the whole world can see it." She looked at Finn, her plan forming. "We need a body camera, small enough to be hidden. A portable hotspot with a secure, encrypted signal. Finn, I need you to set up a private, live-streaming link and have it ready to go public with a single click. I'm not just going to get a confession; I'm going to make the whole world the witness."

She was no longer the girl who ran. She was a woman gathering her strength for one final, desperate battle.

As if summoned by her decision, her phone, which had been silent for hours, buzzed in her pocket. It was a text from an unknown number. Her blood ran cold, but she felt no fear, only a strange, chilling sense of destiny.

The voice was unmistakable.

You wanted to finish Sarah's story, Julia. Come to the cliffs at dawn. Alone. Let's write the ending together.

It was him. The mastermind. And he was summoning her to the final battlefield. The place where it all began, and the place where, one way or another, it was all about to end.

Chapter 16: The Final Confession

Dawn at the cliffs was a raw, brutal affair. A sliver of pale, bloody light bled across the horizon, illuminating a world of grey mist and churning, slate-colored water. The wind howled, a ceaseless, mournful cry that ripped at Julia's clothes and stung her eyes with salt spray. It was the edge of the world, the place where Sarah's story had ended. The place where Julia would write the final chapter.

She was wired. A tiny, button-sized camera was pinned to her jacket, the live feed going directly to Finn, who was parked a mile down the road, ready to unleash the truth with a single click. Every nerve in her body was a live wire, a taut string of terror and adrenaline. She was walking into a trap, but she had turned it into her stage.

She saw them waiting for her near the gnarled cypress tree. Mayor Evelyn Crane stood with her back to the sea, a picture of aristocratic calm. Beside her, a grim-faced Clayton Ward stood like a monolith.

"Julia," Evelyn said, her voice smooth and devoid of warmth. "I'm so glad you decided to be reasonable."

"Where is he?" Julia demanded.

Evelyn smiled, a thin, cruel expression, and held up her phone. The screen showed a picture of Alec, bound to a chair in a dark room, his face bruised but defiant. "Your knight is safe. For now. Give me the ledgers Sarah hid here, and I will give you back your broken detective."

"Why?" Julia asked, stalling, letting the camera drink in every detail. "Why go to all this trouble for a decade-old mistake?"

"Christopher was a disappointment," Evelyn spat, her voice dripping with disdain. "He didn't even mean to kill her. He had a tantrum, she fell, and he stood there crying over her body like a child. I had to handle it. I've always had to handle the messes of weak men. My father built an empire on this land, and I wasn't about to let a fisherman's daughter threaten my birthright."

It was all there. The confession, cold and remorseless.

"So you silence witnesses, you buy cops, you threaten families... all for a payday?"

"For what is rightfully mine!" Evelyn shrieked. "And I will not let you take it!"

"You won't get away with this."

"I already have," Clayton grunted, taking a menacing step forward. "And now, we're done talking."

He lunged for her. But a new voice cut through the wind, sharp and full of fury.

"Get away from her."

Alec. He stood at the edge of the cliff path, his face a mess of cuts and bruises, but his eyes were blazing.

"How?" Evelyn hissed, her composure shattering.

"You left me with a rookie, Evelyn," Alec said, taking a step forward, his eyes burning with cold fire. "A rookie who forgot to check my boots for a lock pick. You left him alone with me for two minutes. That was all the time I needed."

The standoff was electric. It was two on two.

"Get the ledgers!" Evelyn screamed at Clayton. "I'll handle this!"

As Clayton moved toward the cypress tree, Alec intercepted him. The two former friends collided with a brutal, violent force. At the same time, Evelyn lunged for Julia, her manicured nails scratching for Julia's eyes. A heavy gold ring on her finger caught Julia's cheek, drawing blood. She fought like a cornered animal, all ruthless pragmatism and privilege, trying to wrestle Julia toward the cliff's edge.

Nearby, Clayton, fueled by desperation, gained the upper hand, pinning a struggling Alec to the ground. He raised a jagged rock, ready to bring it down on Alec's head.

At that same moment, Julia, still grappling with Evelyn for the ledger she had just unearthed from beneath the tree's roots, saw the danger. With a surge of adrenaline, she kicked out with her free leg, sending a shower of loose shale and stones skittering across the ground. The unexpected spray of rocks hit Clayton's shins, making him cry out and lose his balance for a crucial second.

It was the only opening Alec needed. He twisted, using Clayton's momentum against him, and ended the fight with a single, decisive blow.

Julia, in turn, used her own leverage, pivoting and sending Evelyn sprawling to the ground. She stood over her, the ledger in one hand, her phone in the other. She held the phone up, the screen bright in the dawn light. On it, a video was streaming, with a viewer count that was climbing into the hundreds.

"It's over, Evelyn," Julia said, her voice clear and ringing with triumph above the wind. "Every confession. Every threat. It's been broadcasting live for the last ten minutes."

Evelyn stared at the phone, her face collapsing from rage into utter, abject horror. Behind her, Clayton, dazed and defeated, looked up and saw the screen. The fight drained out of him, replaced by the blank, slack-jawed expression of a man whose entire world has just evaporated. He didn't just look beaten; he looked erased.

At that same moment, the first wail of an approaching siren cut through the air. Not the local police. The sound was different. State troopers.

The sirens grew louder, closer. The sun finally broke free of the horizon, flooding the cliffs with a clean, uncompromising light. It was over. The truth was out. And as Julia and Alec stood together, bruised and battered but unbroken, they watched as justice, long overdue, finally came screaming up the road to Misty Cove.

Chapter 17: Rescue and Reckoning

The dawn that broke over the cliffs was the first one in ten years that didn't feel haunted. It was clean and sharp, the sunlight cutting through the last of the mist, making the rain-washed world glitter. The roar of the fire was gone, replaced by the crackle of official radios and the calm, authoritative voices of the state troopers who now controlled the scene.

Julia and Alec sat on the bumper of an ambulance, wrapped in thick, scratchy blankets. A paramedic had cleaned the cut on Julia's cheek and bandaged Alec's bruised shoulder. The adrenaline had evaporated, leaving behind a bone-deep exhaustion so profound it felt like a state of grace. Every muscle ached. Every nerve felt raw. But they were alive. They were together.

They watched as a defeated, hollow-eyed Evelyn Crane was led in handcuffs to a waiting squad car. A few minutes later, a bruised and broken Clayton Ward followed, his head bowed in a final, pathetic admission of defeat. He didn't look at Alec. He couldn't.

A stern-faced detective with tired eyes and a State Police jacket knelt in front of them. "The D.A. is going to have a field day," he said, a grimly satisfied look on his face. "With that live-stream and the evidence from the boathouse, we'll unravel the entire Crane empire. This goes far beyond one murder in Misty Cove. You did good work, Ms. Hart. Brave work."

Julia just nodded, the words barely registering. She looked at Alec, who was watching the sunrise paint the cove in hues of rose and gold. He met her gaze, and a small, tired smile touched his lips. He reached over and took her hand, his fingers lacing through hers. It was a simple, quiet gesture that said everything. *We did it.*

The ride back into town was surreal. As they crested the hill overlooking the green, they saw a sight Julia hadn't witnessed in a decade: people. They were out on their porches, talking in small, animated groups. The oppressive silence that had suffocated Misty Cove for so long had finally broken.

When the detective's car pulled up in front of the town hall, a small, hesitant crowd gathered. Finn was there, looking like he hadn't slept in a week, and he pulled Julia into a fierce, relieved hug. Grace stood beside him, her eyes shining with proud tears. She looked at Julia, then turned her warm gaze to Alec, placing a gentle hand on his arm.

"Angus Mason would be so proud of the man you are today, Alec," she said softly, her voice thick with emotion. "You brought the truth home."

Julia saw the tension in Alec's shoulders ease, a final, heavy weight lifting from him at Grace's words of absolution.

The townsfolk stepped forward. Mrs. Gable gave Julia a stiff nod. "You did right by that girl," she said. The fisherman who had given her the note appeared, tipping his hat. The whispers that followed her now weren't suspicious; they were grateful. Her work was finally, truly, acknowledged.

Amidst the controlled chaos, Alec guided her to a quiet bench on the far side of the green. They sat in silence for a long time, watching the town slowly, tentatively, come back to life. His guilt, which had been a shroud around him for so long, had not vanished, but it was no longer a crushing weight.

"You were right," he said softly, his gaze on the horizon. "The silence was the poison. You had to be loud to be heard."

"We were loud," she corrected him gently, squeezing his hand. "Together."

He squeezed back, turning to face her. "And whatever comes next, Julia," he said, his voice full of a quiet, steady certainty. "We face it together. No more running."

The future was a blank page, but for the first time, it felt like a promise.

Her phone, which had been silent for hours, began to ring. She looked at the screen. David Chen, the executive editor of the *New York Ledger*. She answered.

"Ms. Hart, David Chen. I won't take much of your time. I just wanted to say that what I saw on that live-stream this morning was the most astonishing piece of journalism I have witnessed in thirty years." His voice was deep and full of respect. "It was brave. It was brilliant. And it was the truth. When you're done there, I want you to fly to New York. I'm offering you a job. National Investigative Correspondent. It's yours if you want it."

It was the call she had been working toward her entire life. It was everything she had ever wanted.

As she stood there, the editor waiting on the line, she heard the sound of a child's laughter from the nearby playground—a sound she hadn't heard once since she'd been back. She felt the solid, warm weight of Alec's hand holding hers. She smelled the clean salt air of the cove, no longer tainted by smoke or secrets. It was the scent of home.

The editor on the other end of the line was waiting for an answer. But for the first time in her life, Julia Hart was silent. She didn't know what to say.

Chapter 18: Letters of Forgiveness

A few days after the chaos on the cliffs, a fragile peace settled over Misty Cove. The state police and the news vans had mostly departed, leaving behind a town blinking in the unfamiliar light of truth. The curfew was lifted. The oppressive silence was gone, replaced by the tentative hum of a community learning to breathe again.

Julia sat on the front porch of her mother's house, a laptop open on the wicker table beside her. It was a tranquil evening, the air sweet with the scent of late-blooming roses and the familiar, comforting tang of the sea. She had fielded the call from David Chen, politely asking for a week to consider his incredible offer. The choice loomed over her, a crossroads between the life she had built and the one she had just reclaimed.

She wasn't writing a news story. She was penning an open letter to the people of Misty Cove. Her biggest story, the one that mattered most, wasn't in New York. It was right here. She typed the final lines.

And so I will stay. Not to chase old ghosts, but to help build a new future on a foundation of truth. This town is not a place to escape from; it is a place to fight for. This is my home. This is my story. And it is far from over.

She hit 'send', submitting it to the *Misty Cove Herald*. The decision felt quiet, simple, and absolutely right.

The soft creak of the porch steps announced Alec's arrival. He moved with a quiet ease now, the haunted energy that had always clung to him finally gone. He sat in the chair beside her, and they shared the peaceful silence of the twilight.

After a moment, he cleared his throat. "I have something I want you to hear," he said, pulling a folded, worn piece of paper from his pocket. It was a letter addressed to Sarah's parents, written a decade ago. He began to read aloud, his voice thick with the weight of his confession—his guilt, his shame, his unending regret for failing them.

When he finished, the paper trembling in his hand, he looked up, his eyes full of unshed tears, unable to meet hers.

"You don't have to carry that anymore, Alec," Julia whispered, her voice thick with emotion. She moved her chair closer and took the letter from his hand, setting it aside. "I forgive you. We were just kids, caught in a storm. It's time to let her rest now. Together."

It was the absolution he had never allowed himself. Only then did she take his face in her hands and kiss him. It was a kiss of profound tenderness, a quiet acceptance of all his broken pieces. He wrapped his arms around her, a silent, shuddering embrace that said more than words ever could.

"It's time for some good news, I think," a gentle voice said. Grace stood at the bottom of the porch steps, holding a small bundle of mail tied with twine. "These have been arriving all day. For both of you."

They sat together as the last of the sun's golden light faded from the sky and opened the letters. The first was from Sarah's parents, a beautifully written note of gratitude that left them all speechless. Alec picked up another letter, written on simple, lined paper.

"'My father sold his boat last year,'" he read softly. "'He thought the cove was cursed. Now he knows it was just poisoned. Thank you for giving him back his peace.' It was signed by a family they didn't know, but a family they had fought for."

"Secrets are like a sickness in the bones of a place," Grace reflected, looking out at the town as the first stars began to appear. "But the truth... the truth is the cure. It lets you heal."

As Grace got up to leave, a small car she didn't recognize pulled up to the curb. A young woman got out, perhaps in her early twenties, with Sarah's same dark, curly hair and a hesitant, shy smile. In her hands, she held a small, framed charcoal sketch of a single seabird in flight. It was rendered with a skill that was both familiar and heartbreaking.

She walked slowly up the path to the porch. "Julia Hart?"

Julia stood up, a lump forming in her throat. She knew, instantly, who this was.

"I'm Hannah," the young woman said. "I'm Sarah's sister. My parents told me what you did. I... I just wanted to come and thank you." She held out the framed drawing. "My mom and dad, they wanted you to have this. It was the last one she drew."

Chapter 19: Sunrise Over the Cove

T he sky over the cove was a soft, bruised purple, just beginning to yield to the tender blush of dawn. A gentle breeze, clean and cool, whispered through the sea grass, carrying the promise of a new day. One by one, then in small, quiet groups, the people of Misty Cove emerged from their homes and made their way to the shore.

There were no official announcements, no formal invitations. It was a gathering born of a collective, unspoken need to witness the first sunrise of their new era together.

Julia stood near the water's edge, the framed sketch of the seabird from Hannah clutched in her hand. Alec was a solid, warm presence beside her, his arm wrapped securely around her shoulders. Nearby, Finn stood with Grace, and

Sarah's parents, the lines of grief on their faces softened for the first time by a fragile peace. Hannah, Sarah's sister, stood with them, her hand finding Julia's and giving it a grateful squeeze.

As the sun finally broke free of the horizon, casting a brilliant, golden path across the water, people began to move forward. They laid wildflowers and painted stones at the base of a large piece of driftwood, creating a spontaneous, beautiful memorial not just for Sarah, but for all the years the town itself had lost to the shadows.

Grace turned to Julia. "They need to hear from you, dear," she said softly.

Julia's heart pounded, but she nodded. She walked to the makeshift memorial, the eyes of the entire town on her. She took a deep breath, the salt air steadying her.

"We have been a town of secrets for a long time," she began, her voice clear and strong. "We let silence become a wall between us, and we let fear become our foundation. I know, because I was one of the ones who ran from it." She paused, her gaze sweeping over the crowd. "But the silence was never as strong as the truth. And the fear was never as strong as the love this community has for its own. Sarah Jenkins was a daughter of Misty Cove. And the truth of what happened to her has finally set us all free."

She placed Sarah's drawing of the seabird at the heart of the memorial. "She is not a ghost to be feared, but a memory to be honored. A seabird, finally free to fly."

As Julia stepped back into the crowd, Hannah met her, her eyes shining with tears. "Thank you," Hannah whispered, clutching Julia's hand. "For so long, she was just the girl who was lost. You gave us back the sister we remembered."

A quiet, heartfelt applause rippled through the crowd. As people began to mingle, sharing coffee and quiet words of hope, the old fisherman who had passed Julia the note approached them. He ignored Julia for a moment and looked directly at Alec, clapping him firmly on the shoulder.

"Your father was a good man, Alec," he said, his voice gruff with emotion. "He'd be damn proud of you. You helped clean the rot out of this cove for good."

Alec, surprised and moved, could only nod. It was a simple gesture, but it was a lifetime of suspicion washed away in a single moment of respect from the town's old guard.

Later, as the gathering was thinning, Alec led Julia a little way down the beach.

"That was the most important story you'll ever tell," he said, his eyes full of a love and pride so deep it made her breath catch.

"I didn't do it alone," she said, leaning her head against his shoulder. "I'm staying, Alec."

"I know," he said, kissing the top of her head. "This is where we belong. Where *we* belong." He gestured toward the marina. "I'm thinking of expanding the business. Hiring a few more people."

"I'm going to take over the *Herald*," she said, the plan feeling more real as she spoke it aloud. "Give this town the local paper it deserves."

They stood there, planning a simple, beautiful future, their individual dreams finally weaving into one.

Finn jogged over to them, his face alight with an idea. "By the way," he grinned, "I heard from a friend of a friend in the D.A.'s office. They're freezing all of the Crane assets. They're not just going to prison; they're losing everything their family stole. The reckoning is real." He then pointed up the coast toward the blackened spot where the boathouse used to be. "I know what to do with it. I'm going to buy that land. Not to rebuild the past, but to build a future. A community center. A place for art, music, a library annex. We'll call it the Jenkins Center. A place of light, right where the darkness used to be."

The idea was perfect, a final, powerful symbol of the town's rebirth.

Later, as Julia and Alec walked hand in hand along the beach, watching the tide wash away the town's collective footprints, she knew with absolute certainty what she had to do next.

"I'm going to write a book," she said, the decision settling over her, quiet and sure. "The whole story. The story of a town that lost its way and then found its way home."

Alec stopped, turning to face her. He smiled, a slow, easy smile that reached all the way to his haunted hazel eyes, finally clearing the shadows for good. "I can't wait to read it."

It was her new beginning. Her new story. And for the first time, she knew, with every fiber of her being, that she was already home.

Chapter 20: The Truth and the Tide

Autumn came to Misty Cove not with a sudden chill, but with a gentle softening of the light. The fierce, windswept days of summer gave way to a tranquil, golden glow that settled over the town like a blessing.

A few months had passed since the morning on the cliffs. The trials were over. The truth, once a violent storm, had become a quiet, settled part of the town's history. The construction of the Jenkins Center on the ashes of the old boathouse was a daily symbol of a community rebuilding itself, beam by hopeful beam.

Julia and Alec walked hand in hand along the beach at low tide, the evening sun casting their long shadows across the damp, glittering sand. The silence between them was easy now, a comfortable and cherished space, no longer a void to be filled with suspicion or pain.

"Finn sent me the final blueprints today," Alec said, his voice a low, happy rumble. "He's adding a small wood-working shop to the center. Wants me to teach a class."

"Will you?" Julia asked, smiling up at him. The haunted look that had lived in his eyes for a decade was gone, replaced by a calm, steady light.

"Only if the town's star reporter and celebrated author has time to cover it for the *Herald*," he teased, his thumb stroking the back of her hand.

Her book, *The Cove of Secrets*, was nearly finished. It was the hardest and most important thing she had ever written. It was a story of crime and corruption, yes, but it was also a story of resilience, of forgiveness, and of a town's long, painful journey home.

They stopped at the water's edge, watching the waves unfurl in lazy, white-capped ribbons across the shore. They could talk about Sarah now, not with the sharp agony of fresh grief, but with a fond, gentle sadness. They spoke of her wild laugh, her terrible taste in music, her fierce, brilliant, and ultimately tragic courage. The past was no longer a ghost that haunted them; it was a part of their foundation, a shared history that had, against all odds, forged their future.

"I finished the sculpture for the mantelpiece," Alec said quietly.

"The one you were working on at the marina?" she asked. "The night of the storm?"

He nodded. "It's a seabird. Like the one in Sarah's drawing. Its wings are spread. It's finally flying free."

Julia's heart filled with a love so profound it felt like the tide itself, swelling within her. She leaned her head against his arm, and they stood in a comfortable, perfect silence, watching the sun dip below the horizon, painting the sky in fiery strokes of orange and violet.

After a long time, they turned to walk back, their path illuminated by the soft evening glow. Julia looked back and saw their footprints, a clear, straight line stretching down the beach. As she watched, a gentle wave slid up the shore, and in its retreat, it washed the sand clean, erasing the marks they had made.

The past could be healed. Wounds could become scars. New paths could be forged. The tide would always come in, washing away the old and leaving the shore new and clean for the morning. All that mattered was who was beside you as you walked forward.

Alec pulled her close, his arm wrapping around her as they walked toward the warm, welcoming lights of the town they had saved, the town that had saved them. The mist was beginning to roll in off the water, but it was different now. It was no longer a shroud, cold and suffocating. It was just the evening fog, a soft, familiar blanket settling over their home.

Sometimes love—and truth—are what remain when the mist clears.

Acknowledgements

A book is never the product of a single mind, and a story like *Shadows at Misty Cove* is no exception. Bringing this world of fog, secrets, and second chances to life would have been impossible without the support, guidance, and patience of some truly wonderful people.

First, I must extend my deepest gratitude to my incredible friends and family, who saw the potential in a cryptic outline and championed this story with a passion that never wavered. And thank you for your sharp eyes and insightful questions; you helped untangle the narrative knots and find the true heart of this mystery. This book is immeasurably better for your wisdom.

My thanks to a friend and retired detective, whose real-world stories of cold cases and small-town justice were an invaluable source of inspiration. Any procedural errors are entirely my own. And to the rugged, misty coastlines of New England, which have always held a special kind of magic and mystery for me.

To my family and friends, thank you for your endless patience during my late-night writing sessions and for tolerating my obsessive ramblings about fictional characters as if they were real. Your encouragement was a constant source of strength.

And to you, the reader. Thank you for stepping into Misty Cove with me. I hope you enjoyed the journey.

About The Author

T revor Jensen is an author of romantic suspense, drawn to the moody landscapes and buried secrets of small coastal towns. He is familiar with fishing villages in Maine, and his writing is heavily inspired by the rugged beauty and quiet resilience of New England. When not at his keyboard, he enjoys hiking and biking. *Shadows at Misty Cove* and he has enjoyed writing this novel.

Find more of his publications at his coming-soon web site at:

http://www.TrevorJensenBooks.com

www.ingramcontent.com/pod-product-compliance
Lightning Source LLC
Chambersburg PA
CBHW031307120726
47906CB00003B/930